Luther Goodyear Bingham

Memoir of Scovell Haynes McCollum, the Little Syracuse Boy

Luther Goodyear Bingham

Memoir of Scovell Haynes McCollum, the Little Syracuse Boy

ISBN/EAN: 9783337310288

Printed in Europe, USA, Canada, Australia, Japan

Cover: Foto ©Raphael Reischuk / pixelio.de

More available books at **www.hansebooks.com**

TRIUMPHS OF GRACE.—FULTON STREET
PRAYER MEETING.

———

MEMOIR

OF

Scovell Haynes McCollum,

THE LITTLE SYRACUSE BOY.

———

VOLUME I.

———

NEW YORK:

BOARD OF PUBLICATION
OF THE
REFORMED PROTESTANT DUTCH CHURCH,
SYNOD'S ROOMS, 61 FRANKLIN STREET.

1861.

INTRODUCTION.

Two volumes published in the latter part of the year 1858, gave an account of the origin of the Fulton Street Prayer Meeting, and made a permanent record of many interesting cases of answers to prayer and conversions which occurred in connection with that meeting. The most of these related to adults. There were even then, however, not a few remarkable illustrations of the power of divine grace as exerted upon the hearts of children, and in after years the number was greatly increased. It has been deemed advisable to collect authentic details in reference to some of these cases, and re-produce them in a series of volumes for the encouragement and instruction of parents and all who wish well to the cause of religion among the young.

The present volume, the first of the series, is devoted to the history of SCOVELL H. McCOLLUM, whose request for the prayers of the Fulton St. Meeting in his own behalf, excited considerable attention when first read, and whose dying exercises when afterwards reported to the meeting and then published through the religious newspapers, awakened a deep interest among Christians throughout the country. The narrative of his training, character, conversion and death is now made complete. It will be found to exhibit a very extraordinary phase of youthful piety. The lad was not prematurely old, nor was there any thing morbid or unnatural in his experience. Yet the gifts of grace, when added to his winning natural traits, made a combination of excellencies such as is not often seen in common life. As such, his biography is here recorded with a view simply to the glory of the Saviour who made him what he was, and to the welfare of others of similar age who may be encouraged to seek and obtain "like precious faith."

No pains have been spared to make the narrative literally exact, even in minute details. The admiring affection which young McCollum inspired in all who knew him may have unconsciously biassed their minds, but the constant endeavor has been to state simply what God wrought, without any embellishment whatever. And the undersigned, although without personal knowledge as to any of the facts related, cheerfully bears witness to the good faith of the compiler, Rev. L. G. Bingham, of New York, and the trust-worthiness of his interesting biography.

TALBOT W. CHAMBERS,

A Minister of the R. P. Dutch (Collegiate) Church, N. Y.

New York, August, 1861.

Transplanted.

A BEAUTIFUL flower has faded prematurely upon its stem, and its little life is gone. It bloomed alone, for it was the only flower — the only off-shoot from the parent stock. It had been, with never wearying care, the object of constant watchfulness. It gave promise of new maturity and fresh beauty. It was lovely to look upon, and the beholder gazed with ever increasing delight. Watchful eyes and tender hands were ever round about it. The choicest culture was bestowed upon it. High hopes were excited in regard to it. The beautiful flower was expected to yield the richest perfume, and bask in perpetual sunshine.

1*

The plant and the beautiful flower were of the Lord's planting, and he had his own purpose in view. Hidden was that purpose for a time. But now it is all revealed.

The flower has been transplanted into the celestial gardens, to bloom forever with unearthly beauty, and flourish evermore in immortal verdure. The unsparing care is needed no longer. The work of tender culture has been rewarded a thousand fold. The heavenly gardens are but a little beyond us, and all the more attractive. There are eyes which long to see them now more than ever. We gaze through the mists of night to catch the first gleams of the morning. Beyond a cold river, we think we see faintly the outlines of the "shining shore." The "sweet fields" are "beyond the swelling floods." Over these "shines one eternal day."

Scovell Haynes McCollum was a boy of
rare endowments both of body and mind.
Such perfection and symmetry of form are
not often met with — added to a face of
great charms and sweetness, with manliness
of manners singular in a child. All these
were coupled with uncommon powers of
mind and qualities of heart. A precious gift
was bestowed when he was given. When
he was removed, a priceless treasure was
taken away. But the glory of God in his
salvation shines above all, and eclipses every
thing else beside.

CHAPTER I.

Compiler's Trip to Canada.

THE MOTHER'S DREAM.

"AND I WILL GIVE HIM THE MORNING STAR." — Rev. 2: 28.

1 METHOUGHT once more to my wishful eye
   My beautiful boy had come;
My sorrow was gone, my cheek was dry,
   And gladness around my home.

2 I saw the form of my dear lost child;
   All kindled with life he came;
And he spake in his own sweet voice and smiled,
   As soon as I called his name.

(9)

CHAPTER I.

THE first idea of compiling the facts which go to make up this volume was conceived by the Board of Publication of the Reformed Protestant Dutch Church. Mr. and Mrs. H. S. McCollum are members of the Church of that denomination under the pastoral care of the Rev. Thomas DeWitt Talmage, in the city of Syracuse. Scovell, the only child of these parents, was thus connected with this branch of the Christian Church. About the middle of March, 1860, he sent a request for prayer in his own behalf to the Fulton Street Prayer Meeting. It was written by himself, and produced a very marked effect in the meeting. It was believed that about that time he was converted. Six months afterward, this boy died. The remarkable, trium-

phant features attendant upon the scenes of
his death bed were published soon after in the
religious newspapers throughout the country,
awakening a general interest in behalf of
children and youth. Great numbers of like
requests began to pour into the meeting, and
the conversion of many, very many children,
was known to follow the reading of the narrative of Scovell's last hours. The interest thus
created continues still.

A knowledge of what the Lord hath
wrought, through the instrumentality of the
most happy and triumphant death of "the
little Syracuse Boy," suggested the importance of gathering up the facts of his history,
and putting them into a more permanent
form. Hence this undertaking. When the
parents of this noble and gifted lad were
first addressed on the subject of a book commemorative of their child, they felt and
manifested great reluctance in regard to it.
They could not bear the thought of giving
such publicity to the events of the little
brief life of their child. They had been
most sorely stricken and much preferred to

keep their griefs hidden from the outside world. They shrank from the observation which such publication would draw upon them, and desired the privilege of mourning their lost treasure alone and unobserved. When, however, they saw how the Lord was using their child's death, as the voice of an Angel Preacher, to bring the children of others to the Saviour, all scruples and hesitation were overcome, and they were willing to lend any assistance in their power to the work.

No pains have been spared to verify the facts herein presented, and it has been a constant aim to state nothing which would not bear the most rigid investigation. Information has been sought by correspondence and personal application, and the compiler desires here to acknowledge the many obligations he is under for prompt answers to letters of inquiry, and for the valuable assistance he has otherwise received. In addition to all other means resorted to, he has made a visit to the home and the birth place of Scovell Haynes McCollum, to the chamber whence

2

his freed spirit went up to God, and to the grave in the beautiful cemetery at St. Catharines, C. W., where his body has been deposited to await the resurrection. He met and had personal conversation with many of the witnesses whose names are given in this book, in St. Catharines, Lockport, Albion and Syracuse, in all of which places the family were favorably known, and the child himself beloved.

The most interesting portion of this visit, of course, was to the place of the final struggle and triumph. We stood beside the bed on which he lay, and before the window at the head of it, out of which he looked upon this, to him, beautiful world. Here in this room, he breathed his last, and here they prepared his body for burial. In this great hall below, they placed the coffin for the funeral. All these rooms, on either hand, were filled with weeping friends and sorrowing mourners. It was out of this door they carried him, and over this verandah, and along this grassy bank beneath the shade of these beautiful trees, and over these pebbly walks where he had been accustomed to play when in health. It was along this street that the sad procession moved to the beautiful cemetery where they laid him away in his last sleep. Here the hand of affection has planted fragrant flowers to adorn his grave, and here, at its head, stands a beautiful marble monument, sacred to his memory, and inscribed on either side with the solemn lessons and messages which fell from his lips, when about crossing the deep waters of death. All this had relation to the mortal part of Scovell.

But there was another part which we went particularly to inquire about. It related to the manner of his death and the triumphs of the hour, of which we had heard so much. We desired to learn from the witnesses in person of those triumphs. We did not know that we should find among those witnesses some with whom we had been acquainted in our boyhood and youth. But so it was. From one of them, Mr. Samson, an elder in the Presbyterian Church, who had been the Sabbath school superintendent, and who had been faithful at Scovell's bed-side and closed his eyes at death, we learned many things which were in corroboration of all that had been written, and some things which were new. He said that no language would describe the ineffable glory that filled the room, and hung around the face of the dying, boy, during the last four days of his life; that if a Christian had only looked into the room and on that beautiful countenance, all radiant, as it was, with unutterable joy, he would need no one to tell him that Scovell's heaven was already begun. "I shall never forget," said Mr. Samson, "the first time I saw him, after he was taken sick. I had understood that the child was very anxious to see me, and I was anxious to see him. I called, though it was against the express orders of the physician that any visitor was allowed to enter the room. But the dear boy was so earnest that his parents could not deny him. I never shall forget the expression of his countenance when his eye met mine. Could you have seen it, such heavenly transport as beamed in his face would have banished all doubt. If I had never seen him again, or heard him speak a word, I should have been satisfied. Such holy joy I had never witnessed before, and never expect again to see shining in any human countenance. At this moment the Doctor entered. Not a word was spoken by the child, and I soon retired."

"One thing was very remarkable," said Mr. Samson; "his whole theme was Jesus, and going to be with Jesus, in all my conversations with him afterward. His views of the way to be saved, though simple, were exceedingly clear and striking. The half has not been and cannot be told. So perfectly happy was he, that he could not bear that any one should shed a tear or be sorrowful in his room. It seemed to be a surprise to him that his friends could weep, or be otherwise than happy. I had never witnessed such a death bed before, and never expect to witness such another."

We inquired of Mr. Samson what were the distinct evidences of Scovell's regeneration—what assurance he had that his ex-

2*

pressions were not the result of education.
His answer was conclusive, and the testimony he presented beyond question or cavil.
We will repeat one of the evidences, because
it will come home to the minds of all who
may read it. For two days, the sick child
suffered almost inconceivably with nausea
at the stomach, and was wrenching and
vomiting almost all the time. Yet not a
word of complaint or murmuring escaped
his lips. Jesus and heaven were his constant
themes of thought and conversation, and invariably, as soon as he ceased vomiting for a
moment, he would return to these themes,
and talk of them with cheerfulness and joy.
"Could that," inquired Mr. Samson, "be the
result of education? Could an unconverted
child of eleven years, under such terrible
suffering, manifest such heavenly joy, and
love to talk only of his Saviour and the
heavenly home which he expected so soon
to enter?"

We had more than one interview with
Miss Linsley, Scovell's drawing teacher, who
we found to be the daughter of old friends,

both father and mother being acquaintances
in early days. From her we gathered support for all the statements which are made in
regard to the nobleness of his character and
the triumph of his last hours. Her interest
in him when a member of her class had
never diminished in his absence. She was a
frequent and welcome visitor at the bed side
of the sufferer, and had won the affection of
the afflicted parents by her delicate attentions,
and the sincerity with which she mourned
with them their great, and so far as worldly
interests are concerned, their irreparable loss.

Rev. Mr. Carey, of the Baptist Church,
St. Catharines, was one who had known.
admired and loved Scovell when in health,
and had visited and ministered to him in his
last sickness. His testimony was like that
of the others—that the half had not been
told, and, more than all, that the whole
could not be told. The glory in that de-
parting soul must have been witnessed to
have been understood and felt. There was a
power in Scovell's death that surpassed any
thing he had ever conceived.

Then there were the household witnesses, the noble old grandfather and the excellent grandmother of Scovell—persons of means, standing and influence in the place in which they have long resided. What would they say? Too full were they to say any thing, though the child had been dead eight months. It seemed but as yesterday, yet all around the house in which he died spoke of the deep distress which his loss had occasioned, and which was just as keenly felt now as ever. The grandfather is an elder of the Presbyterian Church in St. Catharines, and a devoted exemplary Christian. We saw those, who told us of the struggle of this strong man to sustain himself under the deep affliction—how during the child's sickness, he presented the case to his heavenly Father, and besought his fellow Christians, in the prayer meetings and in their closets, to unite with him in earnest entreaty that, if it were God's will, the life of his only grandchild might be spared. His was a profound, an abiding, a lifetime sorrow, and yet he was enabled by Divine grace, while

he mourned none the less, to rejoice in the
realization that God had mingled mercy and
comfort with the affliction, and was over-
ruling all to his glory in the salvation of
so many of the dear children and youth of
our land.

And the father and mother; they had returned again after an absence of eight
months, to weep together at the grave of
their departed child, and to adorn and
beautify his last resting place.   In the chamber where death relieved Scovell from his
bodily sufferings, we conversed with them
of their treasure which they have laid up
in heaven.   Here in the seclusion of this hal-
lowed spot, we had an opportunity to study
the character of the mother who had trained
up her only child in preparation for *such a
death*. Retiring in disposition, and lacking in
self-confidence, she would not be known for
that Christian activity which is seen by the
world, and developed in the more public
labors of the Church. But in the quiet of
home, by the hearth side and the altar, in
the chamber and the closet, the talents God

gave her have been improved, until at length, when he called her to render back the treasure he had committed to her stewardship, she could say, "Here, Lord, am I, and the child whom thou hast given me." She had been a true mother, educating her child in view of all her responsibilities for time and for eternity. Oh! that Christian mothers would feel more of this responsibility — that more of the children of our land might be thus given to God, and prepared by prayer and faith, and true Godly maternal devotion, to shine with Scovell, like stars, in the kingdom of heaven! From other witnesses, we learned of the wonderful composure which this mother exhibited during the last sickness, at the funeral and at the grave. For the child's sake, she suppressed her emotions while he lived, and with calm, heroic, Christian resignation, she saw her treasure consigned to the earth without the shedding of a tear, or an audible expression of the deep grief which weighed so heavily upon her. And yet, in the quiet of her own retirement, while she murmurs not, nor repines, she is wont to give way to her feelings and seek relief in floods of tears. Though, too, she thanks God, day by day, for the gift of such a treasure, and for over-ruling her afflictions to his glory in the conversion of so many of the children and youth of the land, yet it is evident that her health fails under the weight of her sorrow, and she longs continually for that meeting of mother and son, in their heavenly home, where there shall be no more parting, and where they can drink together from those cooling waters of which he so much longed to partake. She seems to feel that her mission is accomplished and her work on earth is ended. May Scovell's God, who has thus far guided and sustained her, still give strength to this stricken mother, to bear up under her afflictions, and comfort and support her as she journeys childless onward through the remaining years of her life; and may He at length, bring her and her dear companion together to that heavenly city where parents and child shall dwell together, without fear of separation for ever more.

An incident which occured on our way to St. Catharines may be here related, to show how widely the death of this lovely boy has exerted an influence upon others. We had crossed the Suspension Bridge, and while seated in a car of the Great Western Railway, a gentleman came along and took a seat beside us.

"Have I not seen you in the Fulton Street Prayer Meeting?" inquired the stranger.

"Very likely," we replied; "when home we are in that meeting every day."

"I thought I recognized you," said he. "Do you remember any thing about the death of a little girl whose case had been mentioned in that meeting?"

We answered that we could not call it to mind. He seemed disappointed, and inquired again:

"Do you remember any thing about a narrative, which was published in the religious papers, of a little girl who died when eleven years old?"

Still we did not remember, and told him that several had been mentioned of late, and we could not distinguish.

"This was under the title," said he, " of 'Father, when will Jesus Come?'"

"Oh yes," we replied, "that narrative is well remembered."

The truth was, we had written and published the narrative from notes taken in the Fulton Street Prayer Meeting, when the case was mentioned there, and we had become deeply interested in it.

"We remember all about it," we continued.

"Well," said he, and the tears started in his eyes, "that was my own little daughter;" [here the tears flowed apace.] "It was my precious little Josephine. Did you ever read the story of Scovell Haynes McCollum?" he added, after a short pause.

"Yes," we said, "we have read the story of Scovell," and immediately both became deeply interested in the conversation.

"You know," said he, "his was a death of glorious Christian triumph. My little Josephine died in the same triumphant manner." Then he went on to tell how the superintendent of Josephine's Sabbath school

3

had read the story of Scovell in the school,
and how it had taken such deep hold on her
tender mind, that it had brought her to trust
in the same Saviour. He repeated the circumstances of that glorious death bed—how
she desired "to see Jesus," to "go to be
with Jesus," and often asked: "Father,
when will Jesus come?"—longing to depart
and be with Christ, which was far better.
When she was told that Jesus would quickly
come, she seemed full of satisfaction and joy.
She called for all her toys and play things to
be laid upon her bed, and with the utmost
composure she apportioned them all out
among her friends. She wished them to be
kept as keepsakes, to remember her by when
she was gone.

When all this was done, she inquired
again, "*Father, when will Jesus come?*"
When assured that he was just at hand, and
she would soon go to be with him, she sent
her last dying messages to her friends, and
bade her father tell them, that when they
should come she would be the first to meet
them as they entered the gates of the celes-

tial city. So she died—kissing all good by, with a heavenly smile upon her face, rejoicing with unspeakable joy that she was going to be with Jesus."

The speaker had been talking through his tears, and saying much more than will be here repeated, in regard to the triumph of the dying hours of his beloved daughter.

"I spent the Sabbath," he continued, "at Niagara Falls yesterday; and I went into a Sabbath school. I was invited to make an address to the scholars, and I told them of the death of my little Josephine. They wept, and I wept, and I hope impressions were made which will lead to the salvation of some souls."

We learned, before we separated, that this gentleman was a member of a Reformed Dutch Church in Brooklyn, and that these facts had occurred at a very recent date.

This is one of the great multitude of children who have been brought, through the eternal Spirit, to repentance and faith in the Lord Jesus Christ, since the publication of the account of Scovell's death.

We regretted that, at Lockport, we were unable to see the Rev. Dr. William C. Wisner, who was absent attending the meeting of General Assembly. Here Scovell was born. Here Dr. Wisner had administered to him the ordinance of baptism. This had been the family home of the child's father for many long years. Here his grandmother McCollum had anxiously and fondly watched his tender infancy. Here her spirit took its departure from earth, and here, in "Cold Spring Cemetery," her body reposes awaiting the call to judgment. Here Scovell had spent the second Sabbath before his sickness, and visited the Sabbath school in which his father had been instructed more than thirty years ago. Here reside the children of his father's cousins, with whom he had played so earnestly the Saturday before, who loved him so dearly, and who were ever so exultant with joy when they heard that Scovell was coming. All around these streets, he had walked and run and played, with his dear companions, with whom he separated for the last time just one week before the hand of disease prostrated him upon the bed of death. With his parents and friends he rode to the Cemetery, during this visit, to look once more at the last resting place of his sainted grandmother, who doubt-less, so soon after, welcomed him to her heavenly abode. Here we met his friends and his parent's friends, and received from them fresh assurance of the wonderful manli-ness and character of the child whose history we were seeking, and renewed evidence of the influence of his triumphant death.

A letter since written by Dr. Wisner, has supplied in part the information and testi-mony we had desired to obtain from him. "My recollections," says he, "of the dear boy are pleasing indeed. I knew him from infan-cy, and can truly say that he was a most remarkable child. His fine form and strongly marked features are ever before me. He possessed a manly beauty which is seldom witnessed in one so young, and there was a peculiar sweetness in his deportment which rendered him unusually attractive and in-teresting. His intellectual and moral faculties were so far developed as to be the subject of

3*

remark and admiration by all who knew him. He possessed a confiding, loving heart, and was strongly attached to his friends. He seemed more the companion than the child, and manifested great interest in themes which would be supposed too elevated to be understood by one of his years. He evinced a wonderful facility to adapt himself to the society he was in. With children of his own age he was as much the boy, engaging in harmless mirth and childish sports, as any of them — in fact, he took the lead in these things, and was looked up to by his young companions as their leader. But when he was with older persons he was sedate, modest, unassuming, and would listen attentively and improvingly to their conversation. His Christian character was truly beautiful. An enlightened and tender conscience seemed ever to control his conduct. Nothing so much distressed him as the consciousness that he had done wrong. He appeared to apprehend with wonderful accuracy the gospel plan of salvation, and to realize most fully that, if saved at all, he must be saved alone by the grace of God. I cannot tell you how much I enjoyed his society during my last visit, but a few weeks before his death, at his father's house, in Syracuse. He seemed more interesting and affectionate than ever. When I came to leave, he pressed me, over and over again, to stay another day; and I have deeply regretted that I did not consent to do so—but business called me away, and I bade dear Scovell a last affectionate farewell. I trust, my dear Brother, we shall soon meet him in heaven, never more to be separated. This is my constant prayer."

We spent a Sabbath in the beautiful village of Albion, and had the privilege of preaching to the congregation with which Mr. and Mrs. McCollum worshiped for four years, and from the pulpit whence Scovell first heard the preached Gospel. We visited the room in which he first attended Sabbath school, and mingled and conversed with those who had known him and his parents. These were the first streets which his little feet were permitted to tread, and here were the associates of his earliest sports. Here,

almost under the eaves of the sanctuary,
stands the beautiful brick gothic cottage—the
house which he first knew as HOME. And as
though conscious of speedy death, and anxious to bid early friends a final farewell, he
had made a visit to these friends and associations, scarce a week before his last sickness.
We can almost see him now in imagination
as others saw him then, his cheeks flushed
with excitement, the perspiration rolling
from his face, and his rich dark brown hair
curling more closely than usual, as he ran
from house to house, now at the back door
to surprise an old play mate, and now, with
more dignity, ringing the bell at the front
entrance to call upon a friend. Scovell lived
in Albion but four, short years, and he was
taken there an infant, but those years were
long enough to form many warm and lasting
attachments among old and young, for he
was only to be known to be loved. While
in Albion, we were a guest of one of the pi-
oneer residents of the village, and one of the
veteran members and officers of the Presbyterian Church — Mr. Harvey Goodrich.

From him and his estimable wife we learned
much of Scovell and his family friends, and
particularly of the sainted grandmother,
whose mortal remains lie mouldering in the
Cold Spring Cemetery at Lockport. She was
with the family some two or three years
while they resided here, and loved Scovell
with an ardor of affection only surpassed by
the self-sacrificing devotion of his mother.
Here, too, we learned of the commencement
of that maternal influence to which we have
elsewhere referred, and of which the reader
will be so fully impressed in the perusal of
these pages. The mother's labors began
when the mind was yet unmoulded, and
before the seeds of wicked influence had
found a lodgment within it.

We stopped a day at Syracuse on our
homeward way. This was the last home of
the boy whose history we sought. From this
city he sent his request to the Fulton Street
Prayer Meeting. Here were his latest school
and childhood associations. We visited the
Sabbath school room where he loved so
to sit under the instruction of his beloved

teacher. The seats occupied by his class
were pointed out to us, and the particular
seat which Scovell was accustomed to call
his own. Every class in the School has a
distinctive name, and a shield. His was
"Robert Raikes Class," and on the wall
hung the shield of the class, draped in mourning for his death. Every inch of the space
in this room had a peculiar interest for the
writer, because here was a place of such
deep interest to this lamented child, gone
now to a higher field of instruction, to be
forever advancing in the knowledge of God,
and to sing songs which grow newer and
sweeter the longer they are sung. We were
indebted to the kindness of Mr. James
Marshall, the loved superintendent of the
school, for this privilege of visiting this
room, and for the information we obtained.
From him, and from Scovell's last teacher,
Judge Spencer, we learned something of the
fruits of his early death and of his dying
message. A few weeks after his decease,
the remaining members of Scovell's class
met, by invitation of their teacher, at his

library, and a class conference and prayer meeting was instituted, which had been held every Sabbath evening since, without a single exception. These meetings have taken the character, mainly, of social and somewhat informal gatherings, led and conducted by the boys themselves, though their teacher is generally with them as an adviser and instructor upon points in reference to which they desire information. They have been meetings of deepest interest. Since their commencement, four of the seven remaining members of the class have been hopefully converted, and upon the first Sabbath in April, they made a public profession of their faith in Jesus Christ, by uniting with the First Presbyterian Church. Three of the four were among Scovell's most intimate companions, and whenever they speak of him, they manifest an abiding appreciation of the virtues of his life, and the triumphs of his death. "His," says Judge Spencer, in a note lying before us as we write, "'t is true, was an early grave, but his entrance upon the life and joys of heaven were alike early. Rather than mourn over the one, we should rejoice at the other, and seek, like him, to strengthen our love to our Saviour, our faith towards God."

Mr. Marshall had also been the beloved teacher of a day select school which Scovell attended, and there was a strong mutual attachment between instructor and pupil. This school was to close on the day after our leaving New York, and we were to be present at the closing exercises. But, by one of those Providences which cannot be foreseen nor guarded against, we were prevented from arriving in time. In these exercises, we were informed, there were often most touching allusions to the bright and beloved school mate whom death had snatched away. Mr. Marshall in his closing address, said: "Death has once entered our circle, and, as has been suggested in some of the compositions, 'once too often.' It has taken from us one who had entwined himself in all our affections. I never fully realized the intimate relations between teacher and scholar until that one was removed. I never lost a friend, the mention of whose name brings up such recollections." The closing hymn, written by a former pupil, for the occasion, contained the following allusion:

"Re-united is our circle;
    Yet we miss some faces dear:
Many now are widely scattered;
    One we shall no more see here.
He was gentle, kind and loving,
    And around our hearts he twined
Tendrils of a sweet affection,
    Which each day shall closer bind."

From Mr. Marshall we gathered much that impressed us deeply as to the general excellence of this boy's character. One marked trait he had noticed in Scovell, which he never saw to such an extent in any other boy. He never appeared to do any thing without seeming to turn it all over in his mind, to see if he had done right. In a moment of excitement, he often did that for which afterwards he was very sorry. When this was the case, he never spared himself, but passed upon his own conduct the sentence of condemnation which his judgment dic-

4

tated. He was by no means a faultless boy;
but never was there a boy more quick to see
his faults or more severe in condemning
them. And this came from his habit of
turning his conduct all over in his mind,
and weighing it well and impartially, in his
moments of calm and sober reflection.

We visited one family where this dear boy
spent much time, running in and out, as at
his own father's house. It was the home of
his bosom companion and one of his dearest
friends, Willie Fitch. There was sunshine
in the face of a young lady member of the
family, as she spoke of the sunshine that constantly beamed in Scovell's. We were informed that not here only, but in every
house where he was acquainted, he was a
welcome visitor, as he was dearly loved by
all his associates.

We were told two incidents in Syracuse,
illustrating the influence of Scovell's death,
and the impression it created among children.
The evening after the sad intelligence was
received, Mrs. Canfield, wife of the Rev. Dr.
Canfield, Pastor of the First Presbyterian

Church, went up to her son Freddy's room, as usual, after he had retired, and found him awake. She talked to him of Scovell, and sought to impress the lessons of his death upon the mind of her child. "I hope, Freddy," said she, "you will pray that Mr. and Mrs. McCollum may be able to bear this great affliction." Freddy took his mother's hand in his, and with streaming eyes, said: "I *have* been praying for them, mother." We were assured that Freddy's prayers were not allowed to go up alone to the mercy seat in behalf of the bereaved parents of Scovell, but that from many a family altar and closet, from many a praying heart, among old and young, fervent and earnest petitions ascended to the great Giver of all good, that they might be sustained in this time of their sore trial and affliction. "Few people know," said Mrs. Canfield to a friend, "how many prayers were offered for these poor stricken parents, or how general and sincere was the sympathy which was manifested for them."

A little child of Mr. Silas F. Smith was

standing by a window, repeating something
to itself in an under tone, which its mother
was unable to understand. Upon questioning it, the child at first hesitated to repeat its
words, but finally told its mother that it was
saying over and over the simple sentence:
"*Every body says Scovell died a Christian.*"
This fact had taken deep hold upon this
young child's mind, and could not be banished from it. God grant that the impression
may be indelible, and that in this young
heart may soon be witnessed another of the
triumphs of grace, such as have been so often
recorded since the first publication of the
narrative of Scovell's death.

Feeling assured that we had failed to
elicit from Mrs. McCollum as much as was
desirable in regard to her method of influence
and instruction of her dear boy, we addressed
to her, after our return to New York, a letter
of inquiry, to which we received the following touching answer. She had no thought
of its publication. Indeed she wrote under
an assurance that we would only use the
facts communicated, and not the communi-

cation itself. But so strongly were we impressed that the letter itself would be eminently suggestive and useful, that we urged her consent that it might be inserted here without emendation or alteration. The consent was, at length, reluctantly given. The letter speaks for itself:

St. Catharines, C. W., June 15, 1861.

Dear Friend:

I thank you from my heart of hearts for all your tender sympathy in my *deep* affliction. In consequence of the interest manifested by you in the death of *my dear boy*, I will endeavor to gratify your desire for a communication from me, with reference to maternal influence. I crave leniency in criticism, as the fabric of ideas will be imperfectly woven, owing to the shattered condition of the mental loom.

When God intrusted to my keeping that blessed child, I felt as if he were a *loan* from heaven, to be rendered back with interest. My daily prayer for him at the throne of grace, if permitted to reach manhood,

4*

was, that he might go forth into the world, as a herald of salvation — thus gathering precious jewels for the Saviour's crown. In my instructions, imparted to him from early infancy, was blended the *one great desire* of my heart—that of seeing him preach the Gospel. God, in his own mysterious way, has answered the mother's prayer.

As the mind and heart of my dear boy expanded, I endeavored to *win* his confidence, and let him *feel* that he had always *one* earthly friend, to whom he could relate his childish trials and sorrows, receiving sympathy in return. Then, too, if he had disobeyed a command, he was instructed *always* to confess it, *without fear of punishment.* These, I consider as furnishing the key stone of that influence ever telling on the heart of my child.

Home, I feel, should be the dearest spot on earth to children. I endeavored, as far as in my power (God knows how oft I erred), to have our's possess a peculiar charm for my boy. A number of hours were daily devoted to him, by way of instruction and

amusemént. My chief enjoyment consisted
in seeing him made happy. I would have
counted no sacrifice too great if it brought
joy to his young heart. Darling Scovell
fully appreciated this. He would give frequent utterance to this expression : " I think
we have such a pleasant home, mamma."
He alluded to it most touchingly in his last
sickness. The happiest hours of my existence
have been passed 'mid the atmosphere of our
own sweet home, " when on a summer eve
we sat 'neath the bower of trees, or on
winter's night, gathered round the quiet
hearth stone." Religion was a familiar
theme upon which we oft held " sweet converse." Every incident connected with his
reading, or transpiring 'mid busy life, was
commented upon, as illustrative of its influence upon the heart, and the importance
of its possession. The name Christian was
to him a household word. I regard this
as a reason why he was not " ashamed of
Jesus," and so oft delighted to talk with
others upon subjects pertaining to Christ and
heaven.

I think that commendation is as grateful to the heart of a child as to those in maturer years. Scovell was often rewarded by being called "Mother's good boy" when he had well performed any duty assigned him. Children, too, need encouragement. Oh! how he leaned on me when a difficult task had been given him at school. Methinks I can hear his sweet voice, as he would often exclaim, when the lessons had been made clear to his mental vision, "I should never be a scholar but for you, mamma."

My heart is pained at the remembrance of the impatience, at times, mingled with his teachings. Oh! if he were with me but *once again* how *gentle* I would be. His little heart should not be *grieved* because mother was "hasty in spirit."

Scovell's heart and mine beat in unison. Our joys and our sorrows commingled. Every thing that interested me, found a responsive chord in his affections. The daily annoyances of life he would endeavor to soothe with his loving sympathy. Do you *wonder* then, that the sun of my earthly happiness set when he was laid in the grave?

When I do thank my heavenly Father for giving me that precious boy, I feel that I did not appreciate the gift, and must ask forgiveness for this great sin.

I rejoice that you remember me at the throne of grace. I, too, would have this great sorrow truly sanctified to me. May it sit like the refiner's fire upon my soul, until made meet for the inheritance of the redeemed.

> " I am weary of loving what passes away;
> The sweetest—the dearest, alas! may not stay.
> I *long* for that land, where these partings are o'er,
> And death and the tomb can divide hearts no more."

Yours, with affection,
S. L. H. McCollum.

CHAPTER II.

Infancy.—Early Childhood.

His Parentage. — Hopes centered in Him. — The Mother begins her Work. — Early Impressions. — Taken to the Sabbath School. — Early Interest and Attention. — Attachment to his School. — Incident. — Love of the Bible. — His Mother reads it to Him. — Love of the Prayer Meeting. — Misdeeds all told to his Mother. — Truthfulness. — Benevolence. — Love for the Aged. — Temperance. — Self-Denial. — Self-Conquest. — Forgiving Spirit. — Syracuse. — Well balanced Character. — Testimony of One who knows.

3 The garb he wore looked heavenly white
   As the feathery snow comes down:
And warm, as it shone in the softened light
   That fell from his dazzling crown.

4 His eye was bright with a joy serene,
   His cheek with a deathless bloom,
That only the eye of my soul hath seen,
   When looking beyond the tomb.

CHAPTER II.

THE subject of this memoir was the only child of Hezekiah S. and S. Luvanne Haynes McCollum, and was born in the village of Lockport, Niagara county, New York, on the 20th day of May, A. D. 1849. He was a descendant of pious ancestors, and in early infancy was dedicated to God in the ordinance of baptism. As soon as his young mind began to comprehend, even partially, what he heard, much time was daily devoted by his mother to reading and telling him scripture stories in simple language, to which he would ever listen with undivided attention. These were always accompanied with instruction adapted to his budding intellect, and sealed with frequent and earnest prayer. Almost from his

·5   (49)

very birth, the good seeds were sown in his heart, which afterwards produced most remarkable fruits of Christian submission and faith. More than once, in his earlier years, when suffering with acute disease, he exhibited these fruits by saying to his sympathizing mother, "It's all right, mamma — God makes me sick."

At a very early age he was taken to the Sabbath school, and soon acquired an attachment for it that never subsided or diminished while he lived. His answers to questions while in the infant department, attracted attention by their promptness, by the distinct voice with which they were spoken, and by the uncommon intelligence and appreciation of the subject considered, which they manifested. Afterwards, when in more advanced classes, he was very rarely without a lesson perfectly learned and fully understood, and he was almost never absent or tardy when not unavoidably detained. He loved the Sabbath school because he loved to learn of God and of heaven; and it was a great grief to him when, for any cause, he was deprived of the privilege of attendance. The particular school to which he was attached was *his* school, and his superintendent and teacher were objects of his warmest affection. Spending, as was always his custom, several weeks each year at the residence of his grandfather Haynes, in St. Catharines, Canada West, he had his regular place in the class in the Presbyterian Sabbath school there, taught by Mr. C. W. Helmes, and almost the first thing he would do upon his arrival, would be to run out and ascertain from some member of the class where was the lesson for the next Sabbath, that he might have it thoroughly prepared. An incident illustrating his attachment to this school, occuring when he was nine years old, may not be deemed out of place just here. His parents were spending the summer at Suspension Bridge, New York, between eleven and twelve miles distant, and desired Scovell to attend Sabbath school at that place. With that arrangement he was not at all pleased, and begged the privilege of going to St. Catharines just one Sabbath more.

The privilege was granted, and he returned
exultingly, exclaiming to his mother: "Now,
I have got to go every Sabbath. I must go.
You wont forbid me now, will you?" He
had sought an appointment as treasurer of
his class, that he might present what he
deemed a conclusive answer to all objections
to the gratification of his wish. The argument prevailed, and, when his parents could
not accompany him, he was permitted to go
by the cars alone to take his place in his
class and discharge his duties as its treasurer.

But Scovell's study of the Scriptures was
not confined to his Sabbath school lessons.
His parents have no memory of the time
when he did not love to have the Bible read
to him; and as soon as he was able to appreciate what it was, he began to delight in
its study, being particularly interested in the
stories of the ministry, sufferings and death
of our Saviour, and in the historical portions
of the Old Testament. During the winter,
before he was seven years old, his mother
commenced to read the Bible through in
course with him, and so earnestly did he

become engaged in it, that he was seldom satisfied unless she read to him six chapters in the morning, and six chapters after he had gone to bed at night. And even after he had heard this number, he would frequently urge her to proceed, saying: "I love it, mamma, better than any story book I ever heard." And such was the deep impression made upon his mind, and such the retentiveness and accuracy of his memory, that, before he had passed his seventh year, the extent of his biblical intelligence would compare favorably with that of a large portion of adult church members. After he began to go regularly to church, he seldom failed to remember the text, and on more than one occasion did he detect and speak of errors made by clergymen in the pulpit, in their scripture quotations. During the pastorate of Rev. Mr. Riggs, at St. Catharines, he was accustomed to instruct a weekly Bible class, composed mainly of Sabbath school teachers. On one or two occasions, Scovell attended with his mother, and answered questions clearly and understandingly which were not

5*

readily apprehended by the older persons present. This fact was a frequent subject of remark, during the after portion of his life, by those who heard his replies, and has been referred to in letters to his parents since his decease.

Scovell was always pleased when permitted to attend a prayer meeting, and would often tell his mother that it was to him the most delightful service of the sanctuary. When at all consistent, his mother never failed to converse and pray with him when he retired to rest at night, and he was always accustomed to offer up his own prayer before going to sleep. In this he seldom omitted the earnest petition: "Write my name *deep* in the Lamb's book of life." Occasionally, when his mother was not with him, he would, at first, forget his evening devotions, but, as he would afterwards inform her, he could not go to sleep until the omission occurred to his mind, when he would say his prayers and immediately fall into sweet and undisturbed slumbers.

Whenever his father was absent, Scovell

always desired to ask a blessing at the table, and was generally permitted to do so. The language he was accustomed to use was simple but expressive. It was: "Oh, Lord God, bless this food to us. Let us not starve or want. Have pity on the poor and give them plenty to eat. I ask it for Christ's sake. Amen."

He was never known to regret the approach of the holy Sabbath, or to wish its hours to pass more hurriedly on. He was scrupulously conscientious in regard to its observance, and was seldom betrayed into any undue merriment upon that day. He always sought for religious reading in books and papers, and, when the *New York Observer* first began to be published as a double sheet, he would usually get it early in the morning, and with a knife separate the secular from the religious department, and lay the former carefully away. If by chance he saw the secular pages in the hands of any member of the family, he would speak to them promptly, but respectfully, of the impropriety of reading worldly articles at that time. If friends were visiting in the family, who were not so particular on that subject, he would often speak to his mother of their writing letters, or reading magazines, or newspapers or books, which he did not consider suitable for the Sabbath, and express surprise that they should have so little regard for the one day in seven that should be devoted to the Lord. How careful ought professors of religion to be of the example they set before children, whose observant eyes and unschooled hearts are ever quick to detect inconsistencies and mark the errors of their seniors.

He delighted in the society of clergymen, and was most happy when they were guests at his father's house, ever seeking their company, that he might converse with them upon topics in which they were interested; never avoiding, but rather desiring, conversation in reference to his immortal soul. When they were leaving, he was always the last to part with them, and always urged them to come again. When in church, if the sermon was earnest, practical and instructive, the preacher was certain of one attentive and appreciative listener, though the language employed was not particularly adapted to the supposed comprehension of childhood.

Scovell's mother was his confidant in all things, and it is believed he never said or thought or did any thing wrong, but that he told her fully and frankly all about it before he slept at night. His anxiety for his mother's health and comfort, his sympathy in all her plans and desires, and his prompt and delicate attention to her wants, were the subject of remark by all who had opportunity to observe them. It is seldom that parent and child are linked together by such oneness of feeling and such reciprocal devotion. But maternal love was not permitted to overcome judgment, and punishment was not withheld when the impulses of youth overcame, as they sometimes did, good resolutions and correct intentions. After his mother had corrected him, he would always put his little arms around her neck, ask her forgiveness, and say, in substance: "Let us kiss and have it all pleasant again, mamma; I can't enjoy myself unless you feel happy." Whenever his feelings became excited, if his mother was patient and gentle with him, as she always was when in health, he would soon become calm, and then with an exhibition of warmest gratitude, exclaim: "You are such a comfort to me, mamma." If mothers would learn from their own experience, or from this incident in Scovell's history, to be gentle with their children, and endeavor to soothe their turbid feelings with soft and pleasant words, they would save themselves many bitter self-upbraidings, when the flowers of their family circle have ceased to bloom in the garden of home. Scovell had a quickness of temper, which would carry him away for a time, but he was extremely sensitive to gentleness, and a few gentle words would generally subdue him. When his temper subsided he always seemed to think over his own conduct and be sorry. If he got angry at his companions in play, and did them injustice, as he sometimes did, he always condemned himself for it, and repented of the wrong, though nothing was said.

Many illustrations of the perfect truthfulness of Scovell's character, and his honor, are recalled by his friends. His grandfather had a rare plant which he was cultivating with great care in his yard at St. Catharines. It had just blossomed for the first time, when the child was passing it, whip in hand, full of play, and the swinging lash clipped the frail flower from the stem. When his grandfather discovered the loss, and began to make inquiry in relation to it, Scovell, who was not before aware of the value of the plant, hastened to confess the act, saying: "Grandpa, I cut it off; I struck it with my whip; I am sorry." At another time, his mother had a daguerreotype of a dear friend, from which the glass had been broken and removed, and she found it one day with the likeness nearly effaced. Upon inquiring who had done the mischief, Scovell, who was in the hall adjoining, quickly exclaimed: "I did it, mamma; I did not know the glass was off, and I thought there was dust upon it."

He was warm-hearted and full of sympathy, especially for the poor, always preferring to go without a meal himself rather than to permit a beggar to be turned away from the door unsupplied. Not unfrequently would he give the lunch he was carrying to school, to some poor child in the street, and himself go hungry until his return home, and often would he ask such children into his mother's kitchen to be warmed and fed, and while there, make special effort, by conversation and delicate attentions, to contribute to their comfort and make them, for the time, to forget their destitution and suffering. He delighted to enter the dwellings of want, and was always a welcome visitor; his tender sympathies being grateful to the inmates, even when he was unable to offer substantial relief. Once, when in St. Catharines, he accompanied a messenger to carry food to a sick and destitute colored woman, who was supplied daily by a few of the neighbors. He was overcome with the evidence of poverty and the lack of comfort, which were presented to his young but observing eyes, and, on his return, solicited and obtained from his mother, a bundle of clothing for the woman and her child, and added thereto the small amount of money in his possession, which had been given him for his own personal gratification. With these he accompanied the messenger the next day to gladden and relieve the needy; and though, in the fullness of his heart, he spoke never a word, the grateful woman afterwards bore testimony that no other visitor had exhibited so much of sympathy and compassion as he. The expression of his large black eyes spoke more of his feelings than words could have uttered. He frequently repeated his visits and his expressions of sympathy, always carrying a ray of sunshine into the abode over which poverty and disease had hung an almost impenetrable cloud.

His sympathy was particularly drawn out towards the family of an industrious man, who had been formerly in his grandfather's employ, but who had been laid aside from active labor, for many long months, by a protracted and painful attack of inflammatory rheumatism. It was always a pleasure to Scovell to carry donations of food or other necessities to them, and usually when meet-

6

ing the wife and mother, he would inquire anxiously for the husband and children, and in the simplicity and honesty of his child heart, would often ask: "Are you warm? Do you have enough to eat?" That mother's heart was touched by the sympathy of the child, and she loves to speak of it, and to express her unfeigned sorrow at his early death.

Not far from his father's residence, some three or four years before his decease, there lived an intelligent and worthy family that had formerly been "well to do in the world," but had been much reduced by successive misfortunes and by the protracted and frequent illness of several of its members. A daughter named Julia, just approaching womanhood, and who had just begun to contribute by her personal exertions to the common store, was *prostrated by disease, and after lingering, helpless and suffering, many long weeks, sunk away and died. During all her sickness, Scovell frequently called to see her, and carried such little delicacies as he could obtain for her comfort and gratification. His grandfather McCollum sent him by letter,

on his eighth birth day, a gold dollar, to
dispose of just as he pleased. As soon as
his eyes beheld it, he exclaimed, addressing
his mother: "I want to take that to Julia
Fuller. Her folks can buy a great many
things with it, and it will do her so much
good." His mother expressed pleasure that
he should' desire thus to dispose of his gift,
and it was not long before his gold dollar
was doing its work of mercy at the bed-side
of the dying girl.

Scovell's respect for the aged was not less
marked than his sympathy and kindness to
the poor. Several instances are remembered
of his gentle and affectionate attention to old
ladies with whom he chanced to meet when
traveling upon rail road trains. He would
always seek their society, endeavor to anticipate their wants, converse sympathetically
and confidingly with them, and offer them,
as the only token of affection at his command, the apples or oranges which had been
purchased for himself.

Scovell's temperance principles were strong
and unyielding. When only seven years of

age, he voluntarily signed a total abstinence pledge, and could never afterwards be induced to taste any intoxicating liquors, even as a medicine, until, during his last sickness, after persistently declining to take it from his mother, he yielded to the earnest request of his physician, and, as a duty, swallowed the prescribed dose of brandy. After listening to an able address by Mr. Sinclair, of Scotland, when he was eight years old, he united with the "Band of Hope" in St. Catharines, and remained a faithful member until his death.

At a very tender age, he was taught to repeat and understand the 32d verse of the 16th chapter of Proverbs: "He that is slow to anger is better than the mighty; and he that ruleth his spirit than he that taketh a city." He was naturally quick and impulsive in his temperament, but would always struggle to overcome his agitation and avoid angry demonstrations. When he had succeeded, he would frequently hasten to his mother, explain to her the circumstances, and exclaim triumphantly: "Mamma, I have taken a city."

When nine years old, after he had been to visit some of his little friends, he said to his mother: "You don't know what a temptation I have resisted this evening. They played cards, and teased me to play too; but I told them No! that my father and mother did not approve of cards, and I would not touch them." At another time, he came home from visiting the same friends, much earlier than was usual. His mother, fearing some disagreement among the children, asked him for an explanation, when she learned that he had left his friends because cards were again introduced. After that, seeing the child's decision and firmness, they never offered to play at cards again when he was present.

Scovell was early made to appreciate the true nature of charity, and to understand that a benevolent spirit, to be at all commendable, should be accompanied by a willingness, if necessary, to make personal sacrifices for its gratification. The disposition of the gold dollar referred to was one illustration of the practical effect of such

6*

instruction, as well as of his natural sympathy and kindness of heart. Another has been furnished by his mother. At one time, he was very anxious to contribute to some charitable object, and voluntarily deprived himself of the use of butter for a considerable time, that he might save thereby the amount he desired to give.

Many incidents might be told to illustrate his forgiving spirit. When at school in Syracuse, the scholars were required to report their standing and deportment for themselves, and in accordance with his habitual regard for system and order, Scovell procured a small blank book, ruled it appropriately, and commenced keeping a regular daily account, according to his best judgment. One of his most intimate play-mates, under the influence of sudden impulse, tore the book in pieces in his presence. He was, of course, greatly grieved, and he could not be persuaded to commence another record; but very soon, the injury was apparently forgotten, and his attachments to his friend were as warm and constant as before. During the examination closing the last term he attended school, his feelings were greatly injured by an unintentional injustice on the part of his teacher; but it was but a few moments after that he was volunteering an act of kindness to him, and the next morning, he was among the most active in procuring a valuable book to be presented as a parting gift, by the scholars, to their instructor.

Soon after Scovell became a resident of Syracuse, an incident occurred which illustrated the frankness and artlessness of his character, at the same time that it proved his respect for his mother's instruction, and his desire to be governed by her advice. During the previous winter, when they would be conversing in anticipation of moving, she would endeavor to impress upon his mind the dangers and temptations incident to city life, and the importance of great care in the formation of new acquaintances. When he had been but two or three days in his new home, he came into the house one evening and said to his mother: "I think I have found a

good boy to play with; he does not swear or
use any bad language." His mother inquired
how he ascertained that fact. "Why," said
he, with the utmost simplicity and honesty,
"I asked him, and I told him my mother was
very particular what boys I associated with."
In answer to an expression of surprise that
he dared to ask such a question of a stranger,
he exclaimed: "How could I find out without?" The boy proved to be all that Scovell
supposed, and they were ever afterwards
warm friends.

It must ever be a rich source of gratification and consolation to Scovell's mother,
that, though the duration of his life did not
reach twelve years, it was long enough to
exhibit such abundant fruits of her prayerful
and unceasing care and instruction. And it
must be a pleasant recollection that the child
fully appreciated her anxieties and attentions,
and often expressed such appreciation in
language like this: "Well, mamma, if I don't
make a good man, it will not be your fault; because you have taken great pains in teaching
me to be good and to do right."

The great secret of the early development of the moral qualities in Scovell's character is to be found in his mother's fidelity.

Scovell always exhibited entire confidence in his earthly parents, and faith in his heavenly Father. When only two and a half years old, a friend of the family was very ill, and Scovell was informed that it was supposed he would die. The child remained quiet a few moments, and then said: "Mamma, Uncle Goodrich wont die; he will get well." "What makes you think so, my child?" inquired his mother. "Because I have asked God to make him well." Oh! the beautiful simplicity of a child's trust! That friend did recover, and lives to offer consolation to the afflicted parents of the child whose prayers were thus made for his recovery.

A few months before his death, Scovell listened with deep interest to a sermon by his pastor, Rev. T. De Witt Talmage, in which the brilliant setting of jewels in our Savior's crown was most eloquently portrayed, and a spiritual application of the

subject most impressively made. Scovell
loved to talk about it afterwards, and when
his mother asked him if he thought he would
ever be one of those bright jewels, he replied
with fullest confidence, but with a gentleness
of manner peculiar to his expressions on such
subjects: "I think I shall, mamma."

Scovell was passionately fond of reading,
and besides the newspapers and books which
he found at home, the public libraries were
used by him to the fullest extent that the
rules would permit. While in Syracuse, he
was accustomed to select and draw books for
himself from the libraries, and it was very
seldom indeed that he brought home any of
the lighter works of fiction. Histories and
biographies were oftenest chosen, and the
former seemed to have a peculiar charm for
his young and expanding intellect. He kept
himself well informed in relation to passing
events, and studied history, partly that he
might the more readily and understandingly
connect and contrast the past with the present.
In his school, he did not consider the lesson
in history a study but a recreation, and it

never required a second reading to be well prepared for recitation.

In reference to Scovell's mental developments, his Christian intelligence and the general balance of his character, all who knew him bear favorable witness. One whose acquaintance was long and intimate, has spoken in language which is quoted below from the funeral discourse preached at St. Catharines, by Rev. Herman C. Riggs:

"God sent him into this world a noble boy. It was not merely the prejudiced partiality of doting parents towards an only child, which ascribed to him uncommon parts. The impartial acquaintance, and the yet more impartial stranger, were impressed with the same conviction. The boy and the man seemed to unite in him, not so as to form that unnatural and unpleasant compound of character, which we not unfrequently discover in the young, but so that his nature seemed to be distinctly double in its development. As a boy, he was remarkably full of the boy's animal spirit and buoyancy. His playmates never found him a whit behind themselves in his tastes for boyish sports. As a youth he was fully true to all the instincts and impulses of youth. He was in every sense *a boy* with boys. But he was more. There was another side to his character, as distinct and marked in its tastes and features as this of which we have just spoken. It led him to enjoy, and often to seek, the society of mature minds. He was an interesting companion for developed men. The thoughtful conversation, and the sober argument, were relished by him. He loved to master the large truth. With an intelligence truly wonderful in one so young, he grappled with many of the theories of mature life, and rested not till he had discovered their foundation, and made them his own. There seemed to be a penetrating power in his thought, which not only demanded for his satisfaction the utmost clearness of view in connection with truth, but which also enabled him to obtain it. Perhaps in no department of truth was this penetration more manifest, than in his apprehension of the facts of revelation, and the conditions of the Gospel. From personal conversations with him on these spiritual themes, I know that many a Christian, whose profession had run through a long life, would have gained by the exchange of his own clouded views of gospel truth for the clear conceptions and statements of this departed boy. His plain understanding of all the essential points of Christian doctrine and Christian faith, as manifested in his forcible expositions of them, was often a source of unfeigned wonder to me. I realized not unfrequently that my experience in these interviews was that of *the teacher taught.* I had at least *received* as well as *given* instruction. Nor is this a solitary experience and testimony. Mature men in every department of life, have joined in the witness of one who knew him well and impartially : 'I never saw so mature a mind in one so young.'

"But mere mental power was not his only excellence. His whole being was warmed by the glow of an affectionate heart. His attachments were ardent and real, continu-

7

ing beyond the hours of actual presence with his friends, and leading to thoughtful consideration of them in their absence. Yet in his warmest friendships, his judgment maintained a remarkable sway over the impulses of his natural feelings, securing a calm and mature regard for those necessities in the condition of others, which might interfere with the gratification of his wishes. In a word, God seems to have centered in him, to an uncommon degree, the elements of power and usefulness in life. All who knew him were led to regard his earthly future as one of fairest promise; were permitted to see the beginnings of powers which, in their ripening, must have fitted him for a large work; the budding of those attractions which, in their full flowering, must have garlanded his life with beauty. But they saw only the beginnings and the buddings. Just as the promise was given,—just as the power began to develop, and to prophesy of its result in the coming years of life, he is cut down."

Scovell's habit of observation and quick perception made him a constant learner wher-

ever he might be.   He knew the number
and name of all locomotives running upon the
roads centering at the place of his residence,
at long sight or by the sound of their whistles,
and was well acquainted with the conductors
on all the trains upon which he was accustomed to travel.   Rev. W. C. Wilkinson,
pastor of a Baptist Church at New Haven,
formerly, while a student, supplied for a time
the Presbyterian pulpit of St. Catharines.
Writing of his acquaintance with Scovell
he says: "Once I remember he met me at
the St. Catharines station.   His cheerful
salutation is in my ear as I write.   He rode
to the town with the driver of the stage, and
I think that he held the reins.   The driver
seemed to be familiar with the youthful
character's appreciation of the privilege, and
apparently delighted to indulge him.   Scovell
amused and astonished me on the way by
the knowledge that he displayed on those
subjects, which boys, I believe, master by
some kind of instinct denied to us older people.   Every horse, every cow, every domes-
tic animal of whatever species, that came in

sight, Scovell would be almost sure to know its peculiarities, its recent history and its present ownership. I mention this as illustrating that the outward hemisphere of his boyhood was not wanting. His physical tastes and appetency seemed to me to be in healthful equipoise with his mental developments."

This same habit of observation led him also to a general understanding of almost all kinds of business, in relation to which he would converse freely when he had opportunity. The last time he crossed the Suspension Bridge, but a few days before his sickness, he was detained with his mother some two hours on the Canada side. Mr. H. Rogers, a gentlemanly and efficient officer of the Canadian customs, who had often before noticed and talked with Scovell, took him into his office, and amused and interested himself in conversation with him. He has often since spoken of the remarkable developments of the child's character, and particularly of his accurate appreciation of the collection of customs and the general rules which govern the business. Mr. Rogers, in a subsequent letter to a friend, speaks of "the affection and admiration I felt for what appeared to me such a picture of nature's work, beauty and intelligence combined in such a high degree and in so marked a manner in one so very young." "When," said he "I heard in full all the beautiful incidents of that death bed scene, though I have been hardened by witnessing many a terrible sight, having been for years in Central India, I felt my eyes moisten, although five minutes previously, I would have said nothing on this earth could bring a tear from me. *I knew the boy and I loved him.*"

In another portion of the letter from which a quotation has before been taken, Rev. Mr. Wilkinson says: "Notwithstanding the brevity of the whole period of our acquaintance, and the infrequency of my meetings with Scovell, and notwithstanding the theory of changes, new scenes and new events since then, I do remember that face and form as if I had seen them yesterday. I attribute this vividness of recollection to the impres-

7*

sion that Scovell's character made upon me. Frank of eye and clear, through its depths, to the bottom of his soul, like the Carribean sea, of a most attractive boyish manliness, saying things that did not strike you as remarkable until you thought of them afterwards in connection with his age, they were so naturally said—the apparently unspoiled object of a household affection that spent itself all on him—evidently a general favorite, yet, so far as I could judge, free from over-weaning vanity or selfishness, cheerful, courteous, dutiful, reverent—Scovell was a type of noble boyhood that I am heartily glad I could not forget."

And again: "I shall never forget how much maternal fondness expressed itself in his mother's manner, when she said to me one day, in speaking of the prayer of perfect consecration, that, as often as she tried to offer it, the image of that son would pass between her heart and God. Dear mother, that image, changed to a heavenly resemblance, is no longer a veil to come between you and your Father! Would that we might all have our veils as kindly removed!"

CHAPTER III.

Education.—Habits.

Miss Gregg.—Mother's Teaching.—Aim in Life.—Talent for Drawing. — Miss Linsley. — Loved by his Class Mates. — Manly traits of Character.

---

5 The odor of flowers from the thornless land,
   Where we deem that our blest ones are,
 Seemed borne in his skirts; and his soft right hand
   Was holding a radiant star.

6 His feet, unshod, looked tender and fair,
   As the lily's opening bell,
 Half vailed in a cloud of glory, as there
   Around him in folds it fell.

(79)

CHAPTER III.

When very young, Scovell developed a strong desire to obtain a thorough education. He learned his letters from blocks, and to read easy words, from the "Pictorial Tract Primer," almost unaided. A very frail constitution and repeated and severe attacks of disease, however, prevented his regular and continued attendance at school until after he had attained his tenth year. Before that age, he had occasionally been under instruction a few days at a time, and twice attended, as regularly as his health would permit, during an entire quarter. The last of these two quarters was at La Fayette, Indiana, where he was under the tuition of Miss Harriet Gregg, in the primary department of one of the public schools. Here he studied spelling,

(61)

reading, elementary geography and simple mental arithmetic. He devoted himself to these studies with that degree of energy and ambition which characterized his whole life, and though detained frequently from the school room by sickness, he was first in his class at the close of the term, and received the first prize for recitations and deportment. The effort was too much for his constitution, and was followed, on the night after the concluding exercises, by a painful attack of disease which nearly proved fatal. He was not permitted to resume his place in the school at the commencement of the next term, but pursued his studies, under his mother's instruction, as constantly as his health would permit,

His regard for order and rule had early become fixed as a part of his mental constitution, and he desired his studies at home to be as systematic and regular as when at school. He fixed himself a desk in one corner of the dining room, arranged his books and slate upon it in the neatest and most convenient manner, and went as earnestly at work upon his lessons as though constantly under the eye of a watchful and strict master. Precisely at the appointed moment, he expected his mother to ring the bell for the opening of school. He would obey the summons promptly, and was always in his seat as punctually as though striving most earnestly for a prize for attendance, with a score of ambitious schoolmates. His school, too, must be opened with system and order, and his mother was accustomed to read a portion of Scripture, after which Scovell himself would make an opening prayer. Then he would turn to his books, and devote his undivided attention to his lessons. If he scratched upon his slate, or made any other unnecessary noise, his mother was expected to touch the bell slightly, and he would invariably give instant attention to the signal. Recess was devoted to the most energetic play, but his studies were resumed upon the call of the bell with commendable punctuality. He was then but seven years of age, but his habits of study, regularity, order and promptness, had been already settled, and he required no incentive beyond the ambition which led him to look forward to a life of professional distinction and benevolent or Christian usefulness.

Scovell's mother continued, as her health and his would permit, to instruct him at home until his removal to Syracuse, in 1859. Rev. G. M. W. Carey, of St. Catharines, mentions an incident, illustrating his promptness and punctuality, when thus pursuing his studies under her direction. He met him on a Monday noon at the Passenger depot of the New York Central Rail Road at Suspension Bridge, New York, where the family were staying for a few months. After a somewhat extended and manly conversation, Scovell suddenly exclaimed, with a look at the station clock: "It is time for me to go to school; I must attend to my studies:" and with a polite bow and a cheerful good by, "sailed off," and ran at full speed to the house where he was boarding.

He was ambitious of future distinction,

and was often heard to remark that he should excel in whatever pursuit in life he might finally determine to engage. He aimed at a high position in one of the learned professions, and early announced his determination to prepare either for the pulpit or the bar. His inclination was for the former, but when doubts were expressed to him whether the condition of his throat would ever permit him to preach, his mind would at once turn to the law, and he would usually ask, with great apparent anxiety, "Do n't you think I could be a good man if I was a lawyer? Do n't you think I could be as good and do as much good as Mr. Sampson, at St. Catharines?" Then he would frequently say, "Well, if I am a lawyer, I will be a good one. I will be one of those lawyers that every body will want to employ." His ambition for education and worldly preferments was very great, but always subordinate in his mind to the greater anxiety which was implanted in it, almost in his infancy, to do good. He was anxious to attain a position of professional excellence and influence, that

8

he might become useful as a man and a Christian.

Scovell exhibited a remarkable taste and talent for drawing, which at the age of nine years, he was permitted to cultivate, for a few months, under the instruction of Miss Emma A. Linsley, at St. Catharines, C. W. Here, close attention and care enabled him to make rapid improvement, and the pencil sketches made by him during that time have been much admired and praised. One of them was exhibited at the fair of the Franklin Institute, in Syracuse, in February, 1860, and received a flattering notice in the report of the appropriate committee. When he first sought permission to take lessons of Miss Linsley, his mother expressed to him the fear that it would be "money and time thrown away." She yielded, however, to his wishes, and as, from time to time, his pieces were finished, or so far advanced that he could bring them home for exhibition, he would show them to his mother, and ex-ultantly exclaim: "Now, you don't think it is money thrown away, do you mamma?"

He was a favorite with the drawing class, as elsewhere, and received many evidences of the affection of his teacher and his associates. When he was about to leave them to remove to Syracuse, in the spring of 1859, these evidences were numerous and touching in their character. When he came home from his last attendance with the class, he rushed into the house, exclaiming to his mother: "I have been almost smothered with kisses to day. All the girls wanted to cut curls from my hair to keep, but I told them they could not have them, because they all belonged to my mother, and *you* did not like to have them cut off." After his decease there were no more sincere mourners than they who had been associated with him in his class, and their expressions of sorrow were most tender and affecting. One who was absent on the day of his death, could hardly be reconciled to the fact that she had not been permitted to see him during his sickness, and with streaming eyes, and a heavy heart, she exclaimed: "Oh! how I did love Scovell. I never loved any other boy as I loved him.

He was not like other boys; he was so noble,
so good.　Oh! how I did love him!"

In a private letter to Scovell's mother,
written in February, 1861, Miss Linsley,
after speaking of the interest she had felt in
reading accounts of his death and the death
bed scenes, said: "But, why not give more
details of his life, which I think was no less
remarkable than his death? He was so noble
and conscientious in his every day life; such
clear perceptions had he of right.and wrong,
and so firmly. would he adhere to the right!
Never shall I forget his exemplary conduct
when with me in my drawing class." In
the same and subsequent letters, she gave
several incidents illustrative of his character.
"Sometimes," said she, "I was called out of
my room for a few moments during the hours
of practice. The other pupils, who were some
six and eight years older than he, would take
advantage of my absence to talk and play,
and would endeavor to persuade him to do
so too. But little Scovell, then only nine
years of age, was never known to leave his
drawing or do aught that he would not do

were I present. I have this fact from the pupils themselves. When it was related to me, I was much affected by the incident—perhaps the more so because he was so *exceedingly fond of play*."

Again, she writes: "It is near two years since Scovell was with me, yet the impression he has left on my mind can never be effaced. I think I can even now see his bright manly face, and hear his polite 'Good morning' as he came daily to my room. Would that some friend would portray his character in all its beauty, as an example to others! If he related an incident to me, or described some object, and afterwards learned that he had misapprehended or misstated the facts, he would always take the earliest opportunity to make the proper correction. If I had misjudged another, how quickly he would inform me, even though it might be to his own discredit to have the truth known. For instance, it was my custom to forbid any communication between the members of my class under penalty of being detained after the others were dismissed. I well remember ·

8*

speaking to one of my pupils who I supposed had been whispering, when little Scovell, not willing that another should be unjustly accused for his fault, quickly said: 'It was I that whispered, Miss Linsley, but I forgot myself.'"

In another place she writes: "I shall not soon forget his affection for his teacher and playmates, or his kindness to those in more humble life, and who may have been insulted or despised by his companions. He was kind and respectful not merely to the sons of wealthy parents, and those of interesting appearance, but also to the poor man's child, and those of less pleasing character. Nor was he ashamed to own them as his friends in the presence of his more favored and proud companions. I remember his asking me one day for permission to show his drawing to one of his *poor* friends, and at another time he inquired if he might have one of them sit in my room beside him, to see him practice in drawing. I shall never forget my surprise as well as pleasure, at the interest he manifested for his less favored companion, endeavoring in many ways to make his stay with him pleasant. Though he traveled so much with his parents, and had so many advantages for seeing the world, Scovell never forgot his old playmates in St. Catharines, and when he returned to where they lived, he was at once a boy and a companion with them again, and loved them as ardently as ever."

And again Miss Linsley writes: "Scovell possessed a joyous, happy temperament, and a manly air and grace of manner far in advance of his years. His bright black eye and curly hair, his erect and beautiful form, his intelligent and happy expression of countenance, would attract you, even though a stranger to him. His brilliant mind and beautiful character I cannot portray on paper as I wish; yet they will remain indelibly imprinted on my memory, and I can never cease to rejoice that I knew your beloved but now departed boy."

CHAPTER IV.

Sabbath School.—Syracuse.

CHURCH CONNECTION.—ATTACHMENT TO SCHOOL.—UNWILLING
TO CHANGE.—"ROBERT RAIKES" CLASS.—TEACHERS.—
MISS WRIGHT.—JUDGE SPENCER.—REFORMED DUTCH
MINISTER IN THE PRESBYTERIAN SABBATH SCHOOL.—
ANNIVERSARY MISSIONARY MEETING.—EXERCISES.—
VACATION.—CHOICE OF PLACES IN WHICH TO SPEND IT.—
VACANT SEAT.—NEVER RETURNS.—DESIRE TO DO GOOD.

---

7 I asked him how he was clothed anew,—
　Who circled his head with light,—
And whence he returned to meet my view,
　So calm and heavenly bright.

8 I asked him where he had been so long,
　Away from his mother's care,—
Again to sing me his infant song,
　And to kneel by my side in prayer.

CHAPTER IV.

IMMEDIATELY upon his becoming a resident
of Syracuse, Scovell united himself with the
First Presbyterian Sabbath school, and although his parents subsequently became connected with the Reformed Dutch Church and
Sabbath school, he was never willing to
change. He would go to church in the
morning with them, and at the close of the
service, hasten off to his class nearly half a
mile distant. His first teacher was Miss
Sarah M. Wright, (now Mrs. James Noxon),
who was succeeded by Hon. Israel S. Spencer,
in June, 1860, but a few weeks before Scovell's vacation commenced and he left the
city. The class—"Robert Raikes, No. 16"—
was composed of eight bright and promising
lads, mostly Scovell's associates in his day

school or on the play ground, and was
noticed by visitors for its interesting appearance, and the intelligence manifested in the
recitations and other class exercises. Scovell
was conspicuous among his class mates, and
his answers and questions were more like
what would be expected from a mature adult
Christian than from a boy of ten years.
Judge Spencer, in a recent note on the subject, says: "I never saw him until I met
him in that class. My attention was at once
arrested, not only by the brightness of his
intellect, but by a deep moral sense which
seemed to underlie and to give tone and
character to all his conversation. He had
an uncommon knowledge of the Scriptures,
for one of his early years, and his questions
indicated that his mind dwelt very much
upon the character and office of the Saviour."

Scovell's attachment to his class and his
school was marked and peculiar, and was
manifested at every opportunity. It was
a frequent theme of conversation at home
and with friends who were not residents of
the city, and never would his bright black

eye beam with greater pleasure than when
he heard his school spoken of in terms of
praise. On one occasion, Rev. T. De Witt Talmage, Pastor of the Dutch Church, by invitation, attended the regular quarterly missionary exercises of the Presbyterian school,
on a Sabbath afternoon, and addressed the
scholars. In the evening Scovell was present,
as usual, at the Dutch Church, and scarcely
was the benediction pronounced before he
hastened forward, and ascending the pulpit
stairs, said : "Mr. Talmage, how did you
like our Sunday school ?"

On Tuesday evening, March, 27th, 1860,
the Anniversary Missionary meeting was
held, and the spacious church was filled with
interested spectators. Each class, by a rep-
resentative or otherwise, participated in the
exercises, as their treasurers made their quarterly contributions to the several missionary
funds of the school. Scovell had been
seriously ill, and for some days had not been
able to leave the house, but Miss Wright was
very anxious to have him take a leading
part, and brought the entire class to his

9

home to make the necessary preparations, and practice for the occasion. On the appointed evening, though still suffering with a painful difficulty in his throat, he was taken to the church, and in the proper order, took his place with his class in front of the pulpit. The boys were arranged in a semi-circular form, with Scovell at the head and a little in front, and gave the following brief history of Robert Raikes, with some of the lessons to be drawn from his life and efforts as the founder of Sabbath schools—as prepared for them by their teacher:

Scovell.—Robert Raikes was born in Gloucester, England, in 1735, and died in 1811, at the age of 76 years. "He was a man of great piety, and besides attendance on the ordinary duties of public worship, was long in the habit of frequenting early morning prayers, every week day, at the Cathedral."

Willie Ryckman.—"He followed the example of Christ, who rose a great while before day, and departed into a desert place and there prayed." "Those that seek me early shall find me."

Scovell.—"To him belongs the high distinction of founding Sabbath schools; and the idea of these institutions was first suggested to his mind by witnessing the painful spectacle of youthful dissipation which the streets exhibited on the Lord's day. At that time it had long been a subject of complaint, among farmers and others, that they suffered more from the depredations of the youth *on that day* than on all the rest." What command of our Saviour did Mr. Raikes obey in this act?

Charlie Mosley.—"Go into the highways and hedges and compel them to come in, that my house may be filled."

Scovell.—Our great leader in this glorious cause engaged in the enterprise in 1781, and held his first school in a barn; Christ was born in a manger; Sabbath schools had their origin in a barn.

Charlie Colton.—"Humble yourselves, therefore, under the mighty hand of God, that he may exalt you in due time."

Scovell.—"As might be expected from a person of such devout and eminently Christian character, he was distinguished for his benevolent support of every scheme and institution calculated to advance the interests of humanity."

Levi Lathrop.—"Give and it shall bo given unto you: good measure, pressed down and shaken together, and running over, shall men give unto you." "For with the same measure ye mete withal, it shall be measured unto you again."

Scovell.—"A Sabbath school association was formed for the benefit of the poor children in the metropolis, and Robert Raikes, in consequence of his zeal and merits, was enrolled an honorary member."

George Thompson.—"The path of the just is as the shining light, that shineth more and more unto the perfect day."

Scovell.—"A far higher honor awaited this benevolent gentleman, in its being publicly certified, a long series of years after, that not one of the scholars at his institution in Gloucester, had ever been either in the city or county prisons."

Willie Fitch.—"He who converteth a

sinner from the error of his ways shall save a soul from death and hide a multitude of sins."

Scovell.—My Dear Classmates : The motto and watchword of this man, of whose life we have given a brief sketch, and whose name is the name of our class, was "TRY." Instructed by his example, and encouraged by his success

Let us "*try*" to be prayerful as he was prayerful;
Let us "*try*" to be faithful as he was faithful;
Let us "*try*" to be benevolent as he was benevolent;
Let us "*try*" to be aspiring in the great work, as he was aspiring;
Let us "*try*" to seek the salvation of souls, as he did.

Scovell's intelligent and animated appearance, his distinct enunciation and energetic and graceful manner, made a deep impression upon the minds of the spectators, and many were the inquiries in relation to him by those who had not made his acquaintance and did not know who he was. The interest which had been awakened in him in the Sabbath school was now extended

9*

through the congregation, and after his death, this occasion was often referred to in conversation in relation to his life, character and promise, by those who were present.

In the note from which a quotation has already been made, Judge Spencer remarks: "Our last school before our summer vacation was a particularly interesting one. The time of our lessons was shortened that we might spend more in exchanging words of parting; and warm wishes were expressed by each that we might all be spared during the vacation, and be permitted to return and meet together again as class and teacher. Scovell was particularly cheerful and happy. He said his parents had given him the choice of *two places* to go to, and that he had made his selection. When I heard of his death, I remembered these words, and they seemed to me to have been almost prophetic. Truly, thought I, he had the choice of *two places* to go to, and I rejoiced in the conviction that he had chosen the place in which he would be infinitely happy through the endless ages of eternity. That meeting, mingled with joy and sadness, was our last one. The vacation passed; our school reässembled; our class gathered together beneath the shield bearing its name, 'Robert Raikes;' but SCOVELL came not. His seat was vacant. Regrets for his absence mingled with our first salutations with each other, and we were sad as we said he would be with us no more. His dying message was delivered to the school, and the impression it made, I trust, will be as abiding as it was solemn. We dressed our shield in mourning, and recorded his death in our class book, with a warm tribute to his memory for his many social virtues and Christian graces."

But Scovell was not satisfied with simply attending his .chosen Sabbath school, and selfishly reaping its benefits. So far as his acquaintance would permit, he was an active little missionary, seeking to draw in other children, and watching to see that they were retained in their classes. At St. Catharines he was particularly successful in this respect, and at Syracuse his efforts were not wholly fruitless. His missionary spirit was however more particularly developed in connection with the "Scattergood Mission Sabbath School," superintended by Mr. Marshall, and held in a German church in the south part of the city, about a quarter of a mile from his residence. Here he delighted ever to repair on a Sabbath afternoon, and alone or with a chosen companion, to go about in the neighboring streets, and endeavor to persuade the uncared for children to leave their plays and go with him into the school. Sometimes, too, in the absence of an older and more experienced teacher, he would take charge of a class of the younger boys, and engage in their instruction with a degree of zeal which was at least worthy of commendation. The fund of bible stories with which his mind was stored, his general intelligence, and simple earnest manner, enabled him to interest such little children, and made his selection as a temporary teacher, notwithstanding his extreme youth, eminently proper.

On Sunday, June 30th, 1861, another anniversary of the First Presbyterian Sabbath School, at Syracuse, was celebrated; the exercises having been necessarily deferred for a few weeks. From the "Third Annual Report" of the Superintendent, the following extract is taken:

"During the last year we have been filled with joy and sorrow at events transpired in connection with our schools. Three of our pupils have been removed by death. One in particular we must mention, because his death has been God's opportunity of converting thousands of children to Christ. His name and the facts of his triumphant death in Christ, are as familiar as household words to all the Sunday schools in our land. May Scovell H. McCollum's dying message to this school ever be the watch word of us all, that we may be Christians and meet us all in heaven. * * * * Who of us will be singled out in the coming year as a warning to those left to be ready and ever about our Master's work? We rejoice in this sorrow when we look at school and church records, and see how God has blessed and prospered us. Six boys have been converted and have united with the Church, viz: Henry Starin, William Matteson, William E. Fitch, William Ryckman, John H. Gray and Levi Lathrop. The teacher of four of the young converts—Judge Spencer—reports that they continue to give good evidence that grace has done its work in their hearts. He further says: 'Our class prayer meetings, instituted last season, are still continued, and were never more interesting than now.' Some of these young professors are now actively at work teaching in the Mission school".

CHAPTER V.

𝕰𝖉𝖚𝖈𝖆𝖙𝖎𝖔𝖓.

SYRACUSE.—MR. JAMES MARSHALL.—INTENSITY IN PLAY.—
APPLICATION TO STUDY.—CONSCIENCIOUSNESS.—EARLY
EFFORTS AT COMPOSITION.—EXAMPLES.—AFFECTION FOR
HIS TEACHER.—AFFECTING ILLUSTRATION.—DISAPPOINT-
MENT.—CANNOT SAY "GOOD-BY."—NEVER MEET AGAIN.

---

9 He said, "Sweet mother, the song I sing
    Is not for an earthly ear:
  I touch the harp with a golden string
    For the hosts of heaven to hear.

10 "It was but a gently fleeting breath,
    That severed thy child from thee!
  The fearful shadow, in time, called Death,
    Hath ministered life to me.

CHAPTER V.

In the month of May, 1859, Scovell removed with his parents to Syracuse. In September following, about a year before his death, he entered the select school of Mr. James Marshall, and continued in it until the commencement of the vacation preceding his decease. His affectionate and forgiving disposition, open and frank manner, kind and gentlemanly deportment, and studious habits, soon won for him a place in the esteem and confidence of teacher and schoolmates. His desire for a thorough and systematic education had grown with his growth, and as he had become somewhat less subject to attacks of sickness, he devoted himself earnestly and assiduously, at his desk and at his home, in efforts to master the studies that were assigned to him. He loved to study as he loved to play, and he was ambitious alike to excel in the exercises of the school room and in the out-door sports in which he engaged with his companions. Every moment of his intermissions was fully occupied, and he returned to his seat panting and heated with exercise, his face flushed with excitement and covered with perspiration and dust. He would seem unconscious how earnestly and violently he had played. With a bound he would go to his books, dash into his studies with the same earnestness, and soon become as absorbed as if he had not been at play at all. His teacher has been several times heard to remark, that Scovell could play more in the same length of time than any other boy he had ever known, and he might have truthfully added, that no child who was no farther advanced could learn more in a given time, or more understandingly and accurately than he.

It was the custom of the school for the scholars to give in their own reports for behavior. One of the older girls several times spoke to Scovell's parents of his correct deportment and truthfulness, remarking that, while some of the boys would report themselves "perfect" when they had been whispering and otherwise disobeying the rules, if they supposed Mr. Marshall did not see them, he never would; and as a consequence of his honesty, his standing on the roll was not as high as it ought to be. Scovell was spoken to on the subject one day at the table, and said it was so—that a good many of the scholars did not report correctly, but he always did, even when his infraction of the rules was caused by and the fault of others. To test him, his mother asked why he did not do as others did, and thus obtain his proper credit and standing. He replied with considerable spirit, "Do you think I would tell a lie, mamma, for the sake of a good mark?"

Two of Scovell's compositions, which were read by him at the semi-monthly public exercises, are here given, not so much to exhibit any peculiar talent in that direction, as to indicate the moral and religious bent of his mind:

"THE SABBATH.

It is morning. The bells peal over the valley and are echoed back by the hills. Who does not love to hear the church bells as they ring on a pleasant Sabbath morning? Behold the people coming from every direction to the little church on the lawn. There stands the church, the sacred church where our forefathers knelt in prayer to the Almighty, for their wives and children. Think of that noble band of worshipers who left their homes and crossed the stormy deep that they might have freedom to worship God. Soon the services end, the people leave, and the children alone occupy the seats. It is the Sabbath school. Prayer is offered, the lessons are recited; then they sing some childish hymns, such as:

'I love to have the Sabbath come,' etc.

Then the school ends. See that poor child, neatly clad, as she trips along to her humble home. How bright her eyes shine as she enters and dances up to her grandfather, holding in her hand a little paper. Her grand-

father asks, 'Where did you get it?' and she
replies : 'At the Sunday school.' How
thankful ought we to be for the Sabbath and
the Sabbath school, when we think how
many heathen children there are who never
heard of *this day* or its blessings. Without
the influence of the Christian Sabbath we
should be like those heathen. Even in our
own land, we hear of many who do not ' Remember the Sabbath day to keep it holy.'
May we heed the lessons taught us at the
fireside and by kind and faithful teachers,
about this sacred day. When we are well,
may our seats never be vacant in the church
or the Sabbath school."

"WAR.

Often war carries with it a blessing as
well as a curse. Often war brings the Bible
and Christ. The war which, two or three
years ago, made desolation in India, and de-
stroyed so many of our noble missionaries,
and that brave English General, Havelock,
whose fame is imperishable both as a soldier
and Christian, has brought salvation to In-
10*

dia. The war which so long continued between England and China has ceased. It has opened a large field for missionaries, and the cry is being continually wafted across the ocean for men to come and preach the Gospel. Our own war of the Revolution, though of seven years' duration, and fought by brave men long and well, brought to us freedom to worship God, and made us an independent nation.

We have spoken of a few of the blessings of war, and now we will mention a few of its evils. It brings destruction wherever it goes. It destroys the family circle by leaving wives widows and children orphans. It lays waste cities; it destroys vegetation and robs the public treasury. Then to think of the hardships the poor soldiers have to endure! Whose heart does not go out in sympathy for the brave soldiers of Washington, exposed to the cold winter, scantily clothed and fed, whom the English pursued by the blood from their frozen feet, that stained the snow. It must require great courage to be a soldier. I suppose as long as the world

stands we shall hear of 'wars and rumors of
wars.' Even now Europe is agitated for
fear of war. I hope e're long the prophecies
of the Bible will be fufilled, and peace will
reign triumphant throughout the world."

On the 22d day of June, 1860, the last
public exercises of the spring term of Mr.
Marshall's school, and the last school exercises of any kind in which Scovell was permitted to engage, were held. It was a solemn occasion, in view of the anticipated parting for the vacation season, and as Willie
Matteson, the valedictorian, alluded to the
probability that this would be the last time
that all would meet together in that school
room or on earth—that before another similar anniversary, some one or more of them
might be numbered with the dead—his words
were deeply impressed upon Scovell's mind,
but with little thought that the circle would
so soon be broken by his own death. Afterwards, when speaking of it to his mother, he
exhibited his love for his teacher by alluding
to the emotion that would probably be ex-

hibited at the next anniversary, if, as it was then understood, that would be their final parting from Mr. Marshall and the final close of the school. "I do n't think there will be many dry eyes then," said he, "and I do n't know who will be able to deliver the valedictory." On the occasion referred to, Scovell spoke a piece, wholly original in thought, and nearly so in language, which being his first original declamation and his last school exercise, is here given:

"KNOWLEDGE IS POWER.

Knowledge is one of the great achievements of man. It is the foundation of all other achievements. It is power. Without it, where would be our academies? Where would be our great men, who give us our books of learning? Knowledge of astronomy gave Columbus power over the savages, when he first discovered America, and enabled him to obtain food and good treatment for himself and his sailors. Knowledge of navigation enabled him first to cross the Atlantic ocean and find the new world; and the knowledge he imparted brought emigrants to this country. As a great result of that knowledge, our powerful republic is now one of the most important nations on the globe. Knowledge has recently given Americans great power with the people of Japan, and enabled our government to be the first trading with that before almost unknown country.

Knowledge of science and mechanics gives us power over water and fire, and enables us to make the powerful steam engine to run, buzzing and whizzing, over our rail roads, and to propel our beautiful steam boats on our lakes and rivers, and across the mighty ocean. Knowledge of printing gives us power over knowledge itself, and enables us to scatter it in newspapers and books all over the world. And what has not a knowledge of electricity done since Franklin brought down lightning from the clouds with his kite? Look at the telegraph poles and wires all along our rail roads, and say if a knowledge of electricity is not power. It sends word to our friends a thousand miles away, in a minute, and brings us all the news of places a great way off as soon as it is known there.

But, we cannot obtain knowledge without labor. The great men who have distinguished themselves for their knowledge, have shut themselves out from the world, and deprived themselves of many comforts that they might obtain it; but at last they came out from their seclusion and were an honor to their country. If we want to make men of learning, we must lay the foundation in our youth by studying hard in school. The great man, Dr. Franklin, who though poor, became one of the greatest men in the world, did not obtain his knowledge in a minute, but by patient and hard study. It took him years, yes, many a year, of hard work, to obtain the knowledge which gave him so much power in the world. If *we* expect to get knowledge in any other way, we shall find ourselves entirely mistaken. *He* loved to study, and *we* must love to study. He was determined to make a man in the world, and we must be determined to excel in our studies, if we would have knowledge and power. You may say that he had natural powers of mind, but he may not have had more than we; or

if he had, they never would have given him
knowledge if he had not improved every
opportunity to study.

Every person has talent—even the poor
boy who drives the canal horses.   But some
persons exert themselves more than others,
and extend their fame as scholars through
the world.   Washington put his knowledge
into power by studying the art of war, and
he made himself the greatest man in the
world, and the 'father of his country.'
Knowledge shows its power in every thing
and everywhere.   We must have knowledge
to do any thing, and those who have the most
knowledge can accomplish the most in the
world.   Our parents send us to school that
we may get knowledge, and learn to be
powerful and influential men and women.
Let us remember at all times that 'Knowledge is power;' let us be punctual at our
school, and study hard to obtain all the
knowledge we possibly can, now while we
are young.   When we grow up we shall
have something else to do and no time to
study."

A year afterwards, when engaged in preparing for another closing exercise, Mr. Marshall stated to the school, in reference to this occasion, that when he told the older boys to write original pieces, he did not include Scovell, on account of his youth and the short time he had been in school; but he afterwards came to him, requested the privilege of writing and selected his subject; and his was the best original declamation of them all.

Scovell's manly and erect form, his intelligent countenance and his happy and affectionate expression, were subjects of remark by the spectators. He was happy in the consciousness of his own success in his studies and in his declamation; happy in consequence of the general prosperity and harmony of the school, happy in the prospect of vacation visits and vacation pleasures, and happy in anticipations which were, alas, so soon to be cut off, and which were expressed, when, just after the exercises were closed, he stepped up to his teacher, and enthusiastically exclaimed: "Mr. Marshall, I shall be one of your scholars next year."

In a confidential family letter to his grandfather McCollum, dated on the 17th of July following, Scovell's mother wrote as follows: "His teacher says he will make a splendid scholar, and a very fine speaker. He is very graceful in oratory. I can assure you his parents are gratified with his attainments. Very many encomiums concerning Scovell's mental and personal endowments reach our ears. He attracts the attention of all. I write you *as it is*—not because a parent's heart is delighted with her child. We feel well compensated for all the money expended for his education. Our earnest desire is that he may have health to obtain a finished one, and that our bright anticipations concerning him may be fully realized."

Scovell's affection for his instructor was almost unbounded, and in his eyes, whatever Mr. Marshall did was right. He always defended him against even the insinuation of partiality, and when, for any cause, he was himself punished, by detention, although sometimes he thought it was undeserved, he never was known to censure or complain;

11

but he would often excuse or explain, and say that we would not wonder that Mr. Marshall would make a mistake occasionally, if we could know how many things there were to perplex him in the school.

This affection for Mr. Marshall was most touchingly exhibited a week after the close of the term. Mr. M. boarded in the family of Mr. T. B. Fitch, and Scovell spent Friday, June 29th, with Willie Fitch, at his house. He saw but little of his teacher, however, as he was engaged attending to out-door business. In the afternoon he spoke frequently of his desire to see him, and said he wished he would come before he went home to tea. He was asked to take tea with Willie, but said he thought he must go home, as his mother would want to know where he was by that time. When he returned, his first words were, "Well, I've come back, but I must see Mr. Marshall." He sat on the front steps talking and waiting rather impatiently about two hours, until nearly eight o'clock, frequently asking how soon they thought Mr. M. would come. Mr. Marshall was to leave the city that night to spend a few days with friends, and Scovell, who was himself to leave on the next Tuesday, could hardly be reconciled not to see him again. He arose two or three times to go, but sat down again, saying, "I wonder if Mr. Marshall will not be here pretty soon?" When he thought he could not wait any longer, he asked Willie to bid Mr. M. good-by for him, "and tell him," said he, "that I hope he will have a pleasant time; I hope he will have as pleasant a time as I expect to have." After he had started, he turned round at the gate and said, "Don't forget to bid Mr. Marshall good-by for me," and then ran rapidly home. It was the last opportunity he had, in Syracuse, to express his love for his teacher, and the two never met again on earth. The "good-by" he left for him was his last farewell, and their next friendly greeting will be in that heavenly land where there shall be no more parting, and where both shall be learners at the feet of Jesus.

CHAPTER VI.

Request for Prayer.

Rev. H. C. Riggs.—Interest in his Ministry.—The Letter
of Mr. Riggs.—Its Influence.—Recollections.—Visit
in the Family.—Conversations.—Writes his request
to the Fulton Street Prayer Meeting on the Sabbath.—Mother reproves Him.—Scovell reveals to
her his Letter.—Influence.—Who can tell?

---

11 "My voice in an angel choir I lift,
    And high are the notes we raise;
  I hold the sign of a priceless gift,
    And the Giver, who hath our praise.

12 "'The bright and the morning star' is he,
    Who bringeth eternal day;
  And, mother, he giveth himself to thee,
  · To lighten thine earthly way.

CHAPTER VI.

In the summer and fall of 1857, Scovell spent a few weeks, as usual, in St. Catharines, and for the first time, listened to the preaching of Rev. Herman C. Riggs, the then youthful pastor of the "First Presbyterian Church" at that place. He immediately became very much interested in his preaching, and formed for him a personal attachment that grew and increased until the very moment of his death. After his return to his home, in all the letters that his mother wrote to St. Catharines, he desired to be remembered to the "young preacher," and he often talked about the sermons and repeated the texts he had heard from his lips. Mr. Riggs being informed of the interest he had awakened in the mind of the child, addressed to him the following letter:

(127)

"ST. CATHARINES, NOV. 19TH, 1857.

MY DEAR YOUNG FRIEND: Frequently, since you left our town, have I been pleased to hear, through your grandmother, that you still remember your acquaintance with me. I might give you many reasons why I am pleased at such a remembrance. In the first place, I am very fond of little boys and girls, as probably you inferred, not only from my treatment of you, but also from the picture of a very nice little girl which I have in my possession. As a very natural consequence of this, I am pleased when little boys and girls whom I like are themselves fond of me; and from the fact that you remember me, I am led to believe that you are somewhat fond of me. Am I right in my belief, or am I not?

But this is not all. I have still another reason for being pleased when told that you remember me. It is this: I conclude that if you remember me, you will also remember some things that you have heard me say. Indeed, your grandmother told me the other day that you could repeat several of the texts

from which I preached when you were one
of my listeners. I hope you will never
forget them. Will you try to keep them in
mind? and will you think about them every
day, and try to remember what I said about
them? Will you try too, to understand them
for yourself—to find out what God means
when he speaks such words to you and to
me? Will you take the Bible and find those
texts, and read the chapters in which they
occur, and try to treasure up God's words in
your heart? If you will do all this, shall I
not have a good reason for being pleased?

But, I will give you one other reason. If
you remember me and what you have heard
me say, then I am encouraged to hope that
you will be a good boy and grow up to be a
good man. When you heard me preach, I
was speaking to you just as much as to any
one else. When I said that *all have sinned*,
I meant Scovell as well as his father or
mother. And did I not speak the truth?
Now, just think! Have you never done
any thing that father and mother did not
like? Have no evil thoughts or words been

cherished in your heart or been uttered by
your lips? Ah! yes. No little boy or girl
now lives upon earth who does not daily
commit sin. So you see I was speaking to
you when I said *all* have sinned. And
when I said that none could be saved except
such as trusted in Christ to save them—except such as felt very sorry for their sins,
and confessed them to Christ and asked him
to forgive them—except such as determine
to do wicked things no more, and ask God to
help them to do right—except such as love
Jesus Christ and resolve to do just what he
would have them do, and nothing else;—
when I said all this, I meant that this is the
only way in which Scovell can be saved—
the only way in which *he* can escape from
hell and live in heaven.

Now, my young friend, I wish you would
think of these things. Will you? Jesus
loves you, oh! how tenderly. Will you love
Jesus? Will you go to him and tell him
how sorry you are that you have ever done
wrong, and that you will try to do so no
more? But I cannot write more now. If

you will do all these things, then I shall be *very much* pleased that you remember me. Remember me to your father and mother. Good-by. Your friend,

HERMAN C. RIGGS."

It would be impossible to describe the feelings or the excitement manifested by Scovell upon receipt of this letter, or the interest it awakened in his young heart. It was *his* letter; it had been written expressly to *him;* it was directed to him, and it was all his own. Every day he would open it and look at every page and try to read it. Every day he would bring it to his mother to be read to him several times, and at each separate reading he would apparently become more and more interested in it, and the truths and instruction it was designed to communicate would become more throughly impressed upon his mind. It was seed sown upon good soil, which was to spring up and bear fruit after many days.

During the nearly three years of Scovell's subsequent life, he frequently met Mr. Riggs, and ever exhibited towards him the same ardent attachment which was manifested almost at their first acquaintance. Their conversations were often upon the subject of religion, and the lessons of the letter above given were earnestly enforced on the mind of the child. In reply to a request for a statement of his recollections of these conversations, Mr. R. wrote as follows:

"The general impressions which they left upon my mind are all that seem to obey my memory now, and I regret that I am unable to recall them with sufficient distinctness to warrant attempting to give such a detailed description as you desire. With Scovell, as with all whom I address on the subject of religion, I avoided a formal and set approach. I rather sought to lead him to it in an unstudied, and as I believe, a less repulsive way. Other topics became the stepping stones to this, and willingly he accompanied me in our natural and easy ascent to the great subject. I never found him otherwise than happy, so far as I could judge, in turning his mind to religious themes, when thus introduced; and, as I have before stated, his theoretical knowledge of true religion was always a source of surprise and admiration to me. I scarcely ever left him without feeling that he was not far from the kingdom of God. Indeed, before his last sickness, I entertained at least the approach to a hope that he was already a Christian."

During the winter and spring of 1859 and 1860, Mr. Riggs spent a number of weeks in the family with Scovell, in Syracuse, and during all that time, the subject of practical religion was often the theme of general or more direct conversation between them. It was plainly evident that Scovell's mind was more than usually impressed with the subject and that his heart had begun to sympathize warmly with the clear mental convictions which he had so long manifested. After one of these "delightful conversations," in March, in which the child had been urged to begin at once the life of the Christian, and, with more than usual earnestness, had

12

expressed his desire to do so, Mr. Riggs informed Scovell's father that he was greatly encouraged concerning him, and his hope was strengthened that God's Spirit was at work in the young heart, and that he would soon take a decided stand for Christ.

On the subsequent Sabbath, his mother entered the room where Scovell had been for some time alone, and found him writing. She gently reproved him for thus spending the sacred hours of God's holy day, but he replied; "It is nothing wrong, Mamma, and I will show it to you when I get through." Soon after he called her and read to her the following:

"MARCH 18, 1860.

To the Fulton Street Prayer Meeting.—I have heard that persons might ask for *prayers.* I thought you would be so kind as to pray for me, a little boy of ten years, that I may be converted.

SCOVELL H. McCOLLUM.

Syracuse, N. Y.

P. S.—*Pray* for me every day."

He asked permission of his mother to copy
the request, and to forward it by mail on the
succeeding day, but earnestly besought her
not to inform any other person, not even his
father or Mr. Riggs, of what he had done.
His only anxiety was that it be read in the
Fulton Street Meeting, and that the prayers
offered in accordance with it might result in
his conversion. But his mother thought it
important that the circumstance be known to
those who were in daily intercourse with
him, that they might more understandingly
apply the truth to his mind in their subsequent conversations; and as soon as an opportunity was afforded, she showed the request to his father. Later in the day, Mr.
Riggs came in and said that he had just had
another encouraging talk with Scovell, and
found him even more serious and earnest
and anxious than at their last interview.
The "priceless piece of paper" was then
shown to him, and a solemn and prayerful
consultation was had over it, in reference to
the spiritual interests of its child writer.
In a letter recently written to Scovell's

father, Mr. Riggs alludes to this event as follows:

"Never can I forget the feelings which I had when I first read that beautiful request. It thrilled me as few things ever have. I could not look upon the dear boy after that without thinking of that prayer, and of the pleasures which its utterance sent swelling through heaven. I felt sure that it was honest, and would be answered. And has it not been?"

In another letter, he adds:

"Well do I remember the impressions which my mind received, when, while a visitor at your house, and upon the day of its date, I was permitted to read his simple, earnest request to the 'Fulton Street Prayer Meeting.' Strange, and at that time unaccountable feelings possessed me, as I looked upon that little paper. God has since taught me their significance. Though Scovell knew it not, we witnessed the dropping of that pebble into the great ocean of living influences. Interesting and beautiful as was the act to us, did we, either of us, dream that it would awaken so many circles of power, whose sweet movings would be felt so far from their humble center? Truly, this is the Lord's work! It is marvelous in our eyes! May He perpetuate the influence of that prayer to the hearts of children yet unborn."

CHAPTER VII.

Letter in the Meeting.

---

13 "The race is short to a peaceful goal,
  And He is never afar,
 Who saith of the wise, untiring soul,
  'I will give him the morning star.'

14 "Thy measure of care for me was filled,
  And pure to its crystal top;
 For Faith, with a steady eye, distilled
  And numbered every drop.

(189)

March 13th 1860

To the Fullonet prayer meeting

I have heard that persons
might ask for prayers. I thought
you would be so kind as to pray for
me a little boy of 10 years that I may
be converted.

Lowell 70 — Mc Collum,
Syracuse.
N.Y.

P.S. Pray for me every day.

CHAPTER VII.

The next morning Scovell was anxious to take his letter to the post office as early as possible, and requested his mother to ask his father for a postage stamp. He had none, but said he would bring one when he came home to dinner. The child was unwilling to wait till afternoon, and asked his mother for three cents, saying "I know where they sell stamps, and I can buy one and put it on myself." She had nothing less than a quarter of a dollar, and hesitated to let him have that for fear he would lose it, but he assured her that he would take good care of it and could get the right change. So she gave it to him, and he ran off with happy heart and buoyant step, and soon deposited the precious paper in the letter box, thinking that only

his mother and his God knew its contents.
Never will be forgotten the manifestations of
joy with which he repeated to his only earthly confidant what he had done, and began to
count the hours that would intervene before
his request would be read in Fulton street.
It has been well said that the request itself
was a prayer. Was not every act attending
its preparation and its deposit in the post
office an expression of his earnest desire for
a new heart ?

"Prayer is the soul's sincere desire,
     Uttered or unexpressed ;
 The motion of a hidden fire
     That trembles in the breast.

Prayer is the burden of a sigh,
     The falling of a tear,
 The upward glancing of an eye,
     When none but God is near."

The request came to the Consistory Rooms
on the morning of the 20th of March. It
was brought from the post office, together
with a large number of other letters and re-

quests addressed to the meeting, by a man who daily attends to that duty. All these are carried to the upper room, and are there examined and prepared to be presented to the meeting. Any one who feels an interest to do so, may see them before presentation.

This was by no means the first request presented to the meeting to pray for a child. Many such had been received since the meeting had been established, and many of them had awakened deep interest. The old and regular attendants will remember the request to pray for a little girl in Savannah, Georgia, and the deep sympathy which was exhibited in her behalf by the touching earnestness of the language employed. But, so far as is now known, this was the first request for prayer for a child, written by the child himself. Four or five persons were in the room when ·Scovell's letter was opened by the chairman of the committee, who attends to these requests from day to day.

" A very touching appeal," said he, handing it to a bystander.

"This is very affecting," the reader said, scanning it closely.

"This language is very peculiar and very earnest. How could this little boy's request be better expressed than it is?" said another.

"This is evidently in the little boy's own hand writing, and written without dictation. It is the boy, his hand and his language," said yet another, scrutinizing the paper closely.

At length, the leader of the meeting for the day came to look over the requests, just before the opening. He was a merchant in the city. He was much moved when he read Scovell's little letter. "This is very remarkable" said he, and his eyes filled with tears. He laid this request away by itself.

It is usual in the Fulton Street Prayer Meeting, after singing, reading of the Scripture and one prayer, to read all the requests for the day at the same time, and then call on some one to remember the several cases of supplication, in prayer, immediately following. Scovell's request was not read with the others. Prayer and singing followed the usual reading in the usual order.   When the hour was about half through, the leader arose, holding a single paper in his hand. "Here," said he with deep emotion, scarcely able to command his voice, "is a request of a remarkable character, which I have reserved until now.   It is the request of a little boy ten years old *for himself,* and is evidently in his own hand writing.   The phraseology, too, bears internal evidence of being his own.   It is evidently written by a child *in earnest* to become a Christian."

As he read the little missive, tears rushed into many eyes, and many were noticed putting their handkerchiefs to their faces.   Instantly, after the reading, two or three were on their feet ready to engage in prayer. The first to lead was a clergyman, who had himself been hopefully converted when he was but eleven years of age.   Then followed immediately another clergyman, who is distinguished for his deep sympathy for the young, especially those gathered in our great institutions of education and reform. Then a merchant prayed for this "Syracuse

13

boy," anxious to become a Christian. In every prayer, to the close of the meeting, Scovell's case had special mention. The burden of petition was that this dear little boy might, *that very day*, while they were yet praying for him, be set at liberty from bondage to sin and death, and be introduced at once into the great family of the redeemed, and become a fellow citizen of the saints and of the household of faith—that he might pass from spiritual death to spiritual life by the renewing power of the Holy Spirit, and become a child of God.

Probably no one case was ever presented to the meeting which excited more tender sympathy than that of Scovell. "The little Syracuse boy" was often afterwards mentioned in prayer, and on several occasions, the remembrance of his petition was particularly requested by those whose hearts had been touched by the first reading of his letter, and the evident earnestness of the words of his postscript: "Pray for me every day." No more was heard from him, however, until after his death. The next knowledge the meeting had of him was, that he had joined, as we trust, "the general assembly and Church of the first born, whose names are written in heaven."

But the attendants upon the Fulton street meeting were not left alone to pray for this dear boy. He was daily remembered at home, in the closet and at the family altar, and his case carried with earnest entreaty to the mercy seat. His mother neglected no opportunity to converse and pray with him, and his Christian acquaintances seemed impressed with a renewed anxiety for his conversion. His parents now have no doubt that, if not before a Christian, he was truly converted at about this time, though they have no means of determining the exact day when the great change occurred. He had ever been thoughtful and attentive to the subject of religion, had ever yielded a ready mental assent when its importance was urged upon him, and always on such occasions expressed a desire to be a Christian. This made it more difficult to form a correct judgment in regard to the result of the special manifestations of interest which have been stated. And, besides, his wonderful buoyancy of temperament, his extravagant delight in play, and his excessive "love of fun" still remained, and his parents were not wholly uninfluenced by the common impression that these characteristics, even in a child, are inconsistent with the possession of true love to God and a "new heart." The world had become practically infidel in reference to the conversion of children, and although many marked modifications of his character were discovered, it was even difficult for his mother to reconcile Scovell's boyhood with true religion. For these reasons, he was not encouraged to believe that he was a Christian, and it is probable that, anticipating some great and almost miraculous developement, he never himself knew when his conversion took place, or had full assurance of his acceptance with God, until it was furnished by the Spirit on his sick bed, and grace was given him for the dying hour.

During the months intervening between March and September, there were no marked

developments of Christian experience; nor
are any incidents remembered of a particularly interesting character, indicating any
change in his views or feelings in relation
to the great question of the salvation of
his soul. He continued to be the subject of
earnest prayers by his more immediate Christian friends, and to delight in his mother's
faithful and untiring instruction. He exhibited a growing spirit of kindness and love, de-
veloping an unselfish desire to please those
with whom he was associated; an increasing
amiability of disposition and control over his
naturally quick temper, and an unabating
attachment to the Sabbath school, the Sanctuary, the Bible and the prayer meeting. In
all this, which was then attributed to the ma-
turing influence of increasing years and intelligence, may we not now, in the light
which shines from his death bed, discover
"the peaceable fruits of righteousness?"

Following the concluding school exercises
referred to, was a long summer vacation, during which nearly all of Scovell's desires for
youthful enjoyments, recreations and pleas-
13*

ures were gratified. He was nearly a week at
Skaneateles, rowing upon the beautiful lake,
and swimming and fishing in its waters. He
then went to New York city with his parents,
and there visited the Great Eastern, the Central Park, Greenwood Cemetery, Barnum's
Museum, and many other places of interest.
He left the city with but one regret. The Fulton Street Prayer Meeting, to which he had
sent his own request for prayers, and which
he had learned to love as a sacred and blessed
place, he had not attended. On the day his
parents visited it, he could not go with them,
because he had a previous engagement which
his conscience and his sense of truth and right
would not allow him to disregard. It was a
conflict between duty and personal gratification, and the former prevailed. He hoped
for another opportunity, but his stay was
short, and it was not granted to him. Returning to Syracuse, he remained but a few
days before going to his grandfather Haynes'
at St. Catharines, Canada West, for his annual visit. Here, with the exception of two
or three days spent among friends at Lockport

and Albion, he remained four weeks, in the enjoyment of unalloyed happiness, and realizing all his anticipations. He was very fond of horses, and his desires for riding were gratified. On the last Monday that he expected to spend in St. Catharines, he was out on horseback alone, and when considerable distance from home, the animal, from sudden fright, became unmanageable, and ran with him through the principal streets. Scovell had lost the reins, but remembering the instructions of his grandmother, clung with both hands to the saddle, and retained his seat until the horse stopped at his grandfather's gate. This incident is selected from the many that might be related, because it was so touchingly referred to on his sick bed.

Never was Scovell's health apparently better than through the whole of this vacation. He had been a frail child from his birth, subject to sudden and painful attacks of disease, and his friends had scarcely dared entertain a hope of his growing up to manhood. But, in the spring of 1860, he began to increase in strength as rapidly as he grew in stature. Disease seemed to have taken its departure, and his fond parents were encouraged to lay out for him plans for that complete education which he so much desired, and for a long life of activity and usefulness. In a letter to his grandfather Mc Collum, written on the 17th of July, his mother said: "I am glad to tell you that Scovell was never in better health than at present. He is getting *stout* in body, improving mentally, buoyant in spirits and fond of mischief." And again, in another letter written only five days before the commencement of Scovell's last sickness, his mother wrote as follows: "Scovell is enjoying himself exceedingly well, feasting on fruits of various kinds, and riding horseback every pleasant evening. He rides to the farm daily with his grandfather, and is having a good time generally. He is real stout and healthy. You would hardly know him if you saw him unexpectedly. Father says he never expected to see him so fleshy."

It was almost "peach time" when Scovell's vacation was drawing to a close, and one

week more would give him a rich treat from
the trees in his grandfather's garden. Know-
ing his extravagant fondness for this fruit,
and thinking it would be a great trial for
him to leave just before it began to ripen,
his mother volunteered her consent that he
should remain. But she had misjudged his
feelings, and found that his school had greater attractions for him than the peach trees.

He was unwilling to lose a single lesson,
however great the inducements offered, in
the way of pleasures and enjoyments. "You
may stay if you want to, Mamma," he said,
"but I must go to my school. You can go
with me to the Suspension Bridge and put
me in the care of the conductor, and telegraph
father that I am coming. I can then go without you, and I will not leave my seat until
the cars reach Syracuse. So you need not
be afraid, Mamma." Besides his own desire
to go, he said that to remain would be very
unkind to Mr. Marshall, his much loved
teacher, who was very anxious to have all
his scholars present for classification at the
opening of the term. To a friend who urged

him to stay, he replied with much emphasis, "Do n't you know that I have got to get my education and must be about it?" The rejoinder of his friend seems now almost prophetic — "I hope you will live to get it, Scovell."

His mother yielded to his wishes, and their trunks were being packed to start together for home on Friday, he having himself designated that day, in order, as he said, that "he might have Saturday to gather up his books and run around among his associates," so as to be ready for school on Monday morning. But it was not so to be. Human calculations were to be disappointed by the mysterious providences of God, and Friday found him upon a bed of sickness which proved to be for him a bed of death. His school days on earth were ended, and no more should his teacher and loved companions greet him in their pleasant room; but his education will be completed in that school beyond the skies, where Christ is his teacher, and angels and sanctified spirits will be his school mates forever.

TRIUMPHS OF GRACE.—FULTON STREET
PRAYER MEETING.

MEMOIR

OF

Scovell Haynes McCollum,

THE LITTLE SYRACUSE BOY.

VOLUME II.

NEW YORK:

BOARD OF PUBLICATION
OF THE
REFORMED PROTESTANT DUTCH CHURCH,
SYNOD'S ROOMS, 61 FRANKLIN STREET.

1861.

ENTERED according to Act of Congress, in the year 1861, by

REV. THOMAS C. STRONG,

On behalf of the Board of Publication of the Reformed Protestant Dutch Church in
North America, in the Clerk's Office of the District Court of the United
States for the Southern District of New York.

HOSFORD & KETCHAM,
STATIONERS AND PRINTERS,
57 and 59 William St., N. Y.

CHAPTER VIII.

𝕾𝖎𝖈𝖐𝖓𝖊𝖘𝖘.

---

15 "While thou wast teaching my lips to move,
    And my heart to rise in prayer,
  I learned the way to a world above:
    The home of thy child is there!

16 "The secret prayers thou didst make for me,
    Which only thy God hath known,
  Arose, like sweet incense, holy and free,
    And gathered around his throne.

14*

CHAPTER VIII.

WE come now to the closing period of Scovell's life.

He was attacked on Thursday morning with severe pains in his stomach and bowels, and, though relieved temporarily by the ordinary remedies for such symptoms, hesitated, for the first time, to accompany his grandfather in his daily ride to his farm, about a mile distant. But anxious to gratify every wish of his friends, and as this would be his last opportunity, he invited one of his play mates to go with him, and took his accustomed place in the wagon. During his absence he was unusually quiet, and complained a little of returning pains. Reaching the house again, he felt somewhat better, and spent a little time in the yard with his companion. When his mother came down to dinner, she found him lying on the lounge, where he had been suffering severely, but without complaint and without calling for her, because he supposed she was asleep, and was anxious not to disturb her rest. Medicines were again administered, and he lay down upon his bed and soon fell into an apparently sweet and refreshing sleep, from which he did not awaken for some two or three hours. Soon after he was aroused, the attack was renewed with great severty, and Dr. L. Cross was sent for, and on his arrival, pronounced the child seriously ill, and commenced active treatment, although the disease had not fully developed its type and character. It proved to be inflammation of the bowels, which yielded somewhat to the remedies employed, until, about the tenth day, the physicians and friends thought they had cause to hope for his speedy recovery; and his father left his bed side with confident expectation that, in the course of two or three weeks, at most, he could be safely removed to his home. On the second Wednes-.

day night, however, hemorrhage of the bowels set in, and from that time he failed rapidly until the Sabbath, when death relieved him of his bodily sufferings.

From the time he was prostrated with disease, but when his recovery was confidently anticipated, he talked freely in relation to his situation, and desired a Testament with large print laid upon a stand by his bed side, where he could reach it, and it was his constant companion. He read from it himself when not too weary, and desired it to be read in his hearing a large portion of the time. His mother, though having no serious fears in regard to the issue of the disease, and planning with him his early removal to his home, did not neglect faithful admonition and instruction in reference to death and eternity. On one occasion, after having, at his request, read to him the first and twenty-third Psalms, she repeated that beautiful verse—" Yea, though I walk through the valley of the shadow of death, I will fear no evil: for thou art with me; thy rod and thy staff they comfort me"—and then asked him, " Scovell, do you think you could feel all of that if you were passing through the valley of the shadow of death?" He replied, quietly, but confidently, "I think I would, mamma." "Then, you think you would not be afraid to die?" she repeated. "I think not, mamma." "You are willing, then, that the Lord should do as he pleases with you—let you live or take you to himself?" "I think I am." And equally confident and clear were all his expressions in reference to the future existence and his own relations to it. The twenty-third Psalm was frequently repeated to him every day, after this, while he lived, and he often recited it himself. It would quiet his mind and apparently soothe his pains, when all else failed.

On the second Wednesday afternoon of his sickness, Scovell ate a small piece of peach, which very soon caused renewed distress in his stomach and bowels. His mother, sitting by his bedside, and watching his sufferings, made use of the expression, "My poor dear boy." He immediately turned to her with a pleasant expression of countenance, and replied: "I ain't poor, mamma; I have a good dear mamma and a dear papa, a dear grandma and grandpa, a dear uncle and aunt, a dear Mary, a dear teacher, and a thousand friends, I believe, if I could name them all, and Jesus, too. I do n't think I am *very* poor."

The change in his disease which occurred that evening, was sudden and unexpected, and though it was at once known by the physicians that there was no longer room for hope in his case, the child and his mother were only informed that the symptoms were more unfavorable. In the morning, he was evidently worse, and probably realized more than he expressed of his danger. He desired his father to be telegraphed to, but in language that should not alarm him; but when a reply was received, asking more definite information, and whether he should come, Scovell requested these words to be sent as an answer: "Scovell is very bad, come immediately," Every day before, when his father was not with him, he had dictated the language of messages to be sent to him, and

was always very careful not to create any
unnecessary alarm. When his mother would
read to him a dispatch which she had prepared, after conversing with him, he would
frequently request a change, saying: "I want
to see my father very much, but you know,
mamma, he has got to attend to his business,
and we ought not to ask him to leave it unless it was *very* necessary." Now, however,
he was anxious to have his father by his bed
side, and forgetting his considerations for his
business, he dictated the expressive message
just quoted.

Scovell's regard and anxiety for his mother's health and comfort was constantly exhibited through all of his last sickness. On
the Thursday morning, after the message to
his father had been sent, an aunt coming in
to see him, he said to her: "I wish you
would stay, auntie, and try to cheer up and
comfort my mamma. I do n't want her to
cry, it makes me feel so badly; it pains me
more than all my sickness." Towards evening she called again and told him she would
stay all night, so that his mother could go

to bed and get some rest. He was very much pleased, and, soon after, when the doctor came in, he said to him: "My aunt Maria is going to stay with me to-night, and I am so glad, because she has been very sick herself, and can sympathize with me so much."

It was at this visit that Dr. Cross first plainly informed Mrs. McCollum that there was no possible hope of her child's recovery, and expressed great fear that his father, who was expected at midnight, would not find him alive. Of course, there was no rest for the mother that night. She proceeded at once to impart the painful information to her dying boy. Anticipating her statement, he inquired, "Does the doctor say I must die?" "I am afraid he thinks so, my child," was the cautious reply. It was enough. Comprehending the worst, he clasped his little hands and raised his eyes in prayer for a few moments, and then, as calmly as he would make preparation for a short journey, he called for the doctor first, and then for his friends, and conversed with them freely and earnestly,

15

but without emotion, so far as his own feelings and condition were concerned. He never, through his entire sickness, expresséd a fear of death, and never, from the announcement that he must die, a desire to live. To his physician he said: "Doctor, you say I am going to die. I have prayed the Lord to take my spirit to heaven, and I shall go there." He requested Mr. Gilbert Samson, an elder in the church, to be sent for, and when he came, he said to him: "I am going to die; I am going to be a little angel in heaven." Mr. S. questioned him in relation to the foundation of his hope, and he replied in the simplicity of child-like faith: "Only God and Jesus can save me; Jesus has saved me—he died for me, and I am going to see him. I want you to pray Jesus to take me to himself, and if it is the Lord's will, that I may see my dear father once more before I die." After Mr. S. had prayed with him and taken his leave, he inquired for each member of the household, and said to each individual, "I am going to die; I am going to heaven; I shall be a little angel there; don't weep

for me, but meet me in heaven: kiss me."
To one of his relatives he said, "I want you
to be a Christian," and when he heard the
reply, "I will try," he said, "Nothing is impossible with God." To a colored family
servant to whom he had long been much
attached, he said, "Simon, are you ready to
die *now*?" Upon hearing the reply, "I am
afraid not," "then," said the dying child,
"you must give your heart to Jesus *now*.
Now is the time! Now is the time! Simon,
I want you to meet me in heaven; will
you promise?"

Then his continual prayer was to see his
father once more. He talked freely of his
teacher and friends, and school and playmates, and wished them all to be told that
he died a Christian, and that his desire was
that they should meet him in heaven.—
He spoke calmly in relation to the funeral
arrangements and of the place of his burial,
desiring particularly that his body should be
laid where those of his parents would by and
by rest beside him.

In a conversation with his mother, desir-

ing to comfort her in reference to her anticipated bereavement, he said to her: "When I
get to be a little angel, mamma, I will ask
God to let me come to you, and if he will,
I will often visit you in your dreams." He
told her he was willing to live, if God should
so direct, for the sake of his parents and
friends, and to do good; but for himself, his
only desire was to depart and be with Jesus.
Now he knew he would be safe, but if he
should recover, he did not know what temptations he might fall into, and perhaps he
would be overcome by them.

During the night his anxiety for his mother found frequent expression, and toward
morning he urged his aunt to come and sit
by his bedside during the day, if he should
be alive, in order to relieve her, and give her
an opportunity to obtain sleep and rest, of
which she had been so long deprived. Once,
when she had been persuaded to lie down
for a few moments, he missed her from the
room and inquired for her. Upon being
told where she was, he said, "I am glad;
don't call her." He often expressed great

fear that her fatigues and anxieties in consequence of his sickness would result in her own serious illness, and it was his constant study to relieve her cares and lighten her labors.

At half-past twelve at night his father arrived, and it seemed that the child's last earthly wish had been gratified. When he entered the room, as though impressed with the fear that even a moment's delay might deprive him of the privilege for which he had so earnestly prayed, Scovell did not wait for the usual affectionate greeting, but from the fullness of his soul exclaimed, " Papa, I am going to die, but I shall die a Christian. I think I am a Christian. I lay myself at Jesus' feet and ask him to do as he has a mind to with me." Then he found time for the expression of natural affections, and raising and extending his emaciated arm, he took his father's hand and imprinted upon his lips the kiss of love. For about a half hour, they held sweet converse together, as the little sufferer's strength would permit, and then he appeared to regard his mission in this world as ended,

15*

and to desire only to depart and rest with his Saviour. During that blessed interview, many were the expressions of hope and faith which fell from the lips of that dying child. "Only God and Jesus," said he, "can save me. I love them, and they love me." A little after he said, "I am glad I am going to die a happy death; ain't you, papa?" And when his father had just given him a drink of water, to allay for a moment the raging fever, he said, "I am glad I am going where I can drink a good long draught of the waters of life, of which, if we drink, we shall never be thirsty." "I would like to go to heaven now," said he, "but you and mother want me to stay as long as I can, and I want to for your sakes." He had no expectations of living till morning, and his anxiety for the salvation of his companions found frequent expression in view of his supposed near approach to death. As his mind was called to Rev. Mr. Riggs, he said, "Tell him I have been very sick, and I love God. Tell him to say that I want all my mates to love the Lord, and lay themselves at Jesus' feet."—

His mother stood by during this interview, and as the tears flowed from his parents' eyes, he said, " Do n't cry, papa; don't cry mamma. I don't cry; I love Jesus and he loves me." He then repeated, with his mother, the beautiful Sabbath school hymn :

1 "In the Christian's home in glory,
    There remains a land of rest ;
There my Saviour 's gone before me,
    To fulfill my soul's request ;

        There is rest for the weary,
        There is rest for the weary,
        There is rest for the weary,
         There is rest for you—
        On the other side of Jordan,
        In the sweet fields of Eden,
        Where the tree of life is blooming,
        There is rest for you.

2 He is fitting up my mansion,
    Which eternally shall stand,
For my stay shall not be transient,
    In that holy, happy land,

        There is rest for the weary,
        There is rest for the weary,
        There is rest for the weary,
         There is rest for you—

On the other side of Jordan,
In the sweet fields of Eden,
Where the tree of life is blooming,
There is rest for you.

3 Pain and sickness ne'er shall enter,
   Grief nor woe my lot shall share,
But in that celestial center,
   I a crown of life shall wear;

     There is rest for the weary,
     There is rest for the weary,
     There is rest for the weary,
      There is rest for you —
     On the other side of Jordan,
     In the sweet fields of Eden,
     Where the tree of life is blooming,
     There is rest for you.

4 Sing, O sing, ye heirs of glory;
   Shout your triumphs as you go;
Zion's gates will open for you,
   You shall find an entrance thro.'

     There is rest for the weary,
     There is rest for the weary,
     There is rest for the weary,
      There is rest for you—
     On the other side of Jordan,
     In the sweet fields of Eden,
     Where the tree of life is blooming,
     There is rest for you.

After finishing, he folded his little hands over his bosom and exclaimed, " Yes, rest for me."

During the remainder of the night he slept much of the time, occasionally rousing up and asking a question, or giving brief expressions to his feelings. At a quarter past two he inquired the time, and asked, " How long before I will go home to Jesus?" At 2: 55, he again asked the time. At 3: 15, he again repeated, "Rest for the weary," and then asked, "How long before Jesus will come after me?" At 3: 30, after taking a drink, he said, "I will be glad when I can drink of the fountain of water which never stops—when I can be drinking all the time." At 3: 40, he again asked, "How long before Jesus will come after me?" At 4 o'clock he said he wanted to die. His mother asked him if it was not a hard thing to die. He replied, "No," and then added, "I love you, mamma, dearly, but I love Jesus more; and you want me to, do n't you?" At 4: 10, he said, "I want to go to heaven *now*. I don't want to stay here any longer." A moment

after, he added, "How long before I can go
to Jesus? I hope the Lord will let me go to
Jesus pretty soon." At 4:15, as he partially
aroused, his mother said, "There is rest for
the weary," and he replied, "In heaven." At
5:20, he roused up and asked that he might
have "every thing clean" about him. After
his nurse had made such changes as she
could, he said, "Heaven now! I want to go
to heaven now." At 5:30, he called for his
father, and wanted to kiss him. He said,
"Don't cry, papa, for when I die, I am going
to heaven, which is a great deal better place
than this is." He then called for all the
family friends who were in the house, and
kissed each one. After kissing his mother,
he said to her, "Don't cry, mamma; I feel
good, and you would feel good if you would
not cry, and felt that you were going home
to heaven." A little after, he called again
for his grandfather and uncle, and said to
them, "I am happy; I am going to heaven."
He called his grandmother from the hall, and
wanted the whole family to remain in the
room. He inquired for Dr. Cross, and said,

" How good he has been to me!" He wanted the doctor sent for, but when told that he
had been up all night with the sick, and they
did not like to disturb him, he said, " Tell
him I have gone to heaven." At 5 : 40 he
said, " I wish Christ would come and take
me; I want to go to heaven; I do n't want to
stay here any longer."

At 6 : 45, after a continuous sleep of about
one hour, he roused up and appeared deject-
ed in spirit. He said Christ had left him.—
" He was near me last night, and we had
such a sweet time together He went almost
up to heaven with me, and then some one
came and took him away from me. Why
did not Jesus take me to heaven with him
yesterday when he was so good to me? Why
did that one come and take Christ away from
me? Why did Jesus desert me? Why has
he forsaken me? I have lost my opportunity; I have lost my opportunity. I do love
Jesus, and do want to go to heaven with him,
but why did he not take me yesterday, when
he was so good to me?" His grandmother,
who was standing by, told him to cling to

Jesus, and he replied, "Yes, grandma, I will cling to Jesus; I will cling to him as I clung to the saddle." He prayed earnestly and constantly for a few moments, continually repeating the petition, "Oh God, save me for Christ's sake." His father and mother prayed with him, and his mother read to him the twenty-third Psalm two or three times, after which he appeared much more happy. But the cloud had not yet fully passed from the mind, and a little after, when his mother asked him, "Is Christ with you now, Scovell?" he replied, "I am afraid not." During the brief period of deepest darkness, Scovell's countenance was contorted with anguish, and presented such a picture of despair as no artist could paint upon canvas, and no mortal mind can imagine.

The facts are mentioned here to illustrate the wonderful grace which followed, giving such striking proofs that Scovell was indeed a child of God.

At 7:05, the doctor came in and said that Scovell would probably live twelve and perhaps twenty-four hours. At 7:10, Mr. Sam-

son called, and talked and prayed with and
for him. During the few moments they
were together, Scovell's faith entirely re-
vived, and when asked if he was not afraid
to die, he replied triumphantly, " Oh death,
where is thy sting! Oh grave, where is thy
victory ? "   He had overcome the adversary,
and his countenance again beamed with the
heavenly joy of a ransomed soul, freed from
every doubt, and trusting with child-like faith
in the great Father above.   As soon as Mr.
S. had gone, Scovell called his mother and
said to her, " Mr. Samson did comfort me so
much, mamma."

CHAPTER IX.

Dying Hours---Hours of Triumph.

---

17. " My robe was filled with the perfume sweet,
    To shed upon this world's air,
    As I joyful knelt, at my Saviour's feet,
    For the glorious crown I wear.

18. " In that bright, blissful world of ours,
    The waters of life I drink:
    Behold my feet, as they 've pressed the flowers
    That grow by the fountain's brink ! "

CHAPTER IX.

On Friday morning, telegraphs were sent to friends in various directions, announcing the unfavorable change in the disease, and the certainty of speedy death. Among the others, his grandfather, Joel McCollum, of Hillsdale, Michigan, and Rev. Mr. Riggs, were notified. He had but little hope and no expectation of seeing either of them, though in due time, answer was received from Mr. R. that he would come as soon as possible. He left messages of love for both, and the assurance of his confidence that he should soon be in heaven.

At a little after eight o'clock, Dr. George P. Eddy, of Lewiston, N. Y., called as a family friend, to see Scovell As he approached the bedside, the child said to him,

16*　　　　　　　　　　　　　　(185)

"I am going home to heaven, doctor; I am going to see my Saviour." During the forenoon he was very quiet most of the time, sleeping considerably. Always, when awake, he spoke freely and almost constantly of heaven, and God, and of Jesus his Saviour. He told every person who came to see him that he was going to die and then live with Jesus in heaven. Miss Linsley, his teacher of drawing, called, bid him good-by and kissed him. He told her he was going to heaven—that he loved Jesus, and should see him before to-morrow. He told his mother he was glad he was going first, as it would be much harder to have her go and leave him. When she was weeping, he said to her, "Don't cry, mamma, I'm going to heaven, and it will be only two or three years before you will come too." A letter was received from Rev. Mr. Riggs, written before he heard of the very dangerous character of the disease, covering a message to Scovell: When it was read to him, he said, "Tell Mr. Riggs for me, that I am going to see Jesus—that I have given my heart to him." About half-past one, P. M., Mr. Samson again called and had a very brief but delighful interview with the suffering but happy child. Just as he left, Rev. G. M. W. Carey, pastor of the Baptist Church, also called, (as he had before done during the sickness,) and talked and prayed with Scovell, receiving the same blessed assurances of his faith in Christ and hope of heaven.— "Scovell, are you happy?" asked Mr. C.— "Happy!" replied the child," with an expression of triumphant joy: "I am going to drink of the River of Life, and I shall never thirst again." After a short pause he added, "Pray for me, that Jesus may be with me till I die; and when I die, I may go to be with Jesus." He was now apparently failing rapidly, and was able to converse but very little. At 3: 10, he inquired the time. Afterwards, he lay quiet most of the afternoon. When awake and aroused, his mind was clear, but he seldom spoke except to give a brief answer to a question. He occasionally said, "Oh dear," when the wet cloths, which were necessarily kept about him, made him feel uncomfortable, but he never uttered a word of murmuring or complaint.

From the note book in which the hand of a sorrowing father penciled the incidents and expressions of the last hour of Scovell's life, the following language, written during the evening which all then supposed would be his last, is quoted :

" If his parents know what Christian resignation is, they believe Scovell exhibited it perfectly to-day, as he has done all through his sickness. As the sun was going down upon his last day on earth, his father suggested that a desire he expressed a day or two before be now gratified—that his bed be turned round so that he could look out the window and see the green foliage once more before he died. He expressed a wish to have the sight, but thought it would be too much to move him, and his judgment told him to submit to the deprivation. So he will never see the green leaves and the beautiful sky again, but to-morrow his spirit eye will gaze with rapture upon brighter skies and more beautiful foliage in the heavenly world which he will soon enter. He will be at home with Jesus whom he has loved, and who died for his redemption. Just after half-past seven, Mr. Samson again called. Scovell said to him, "I am going to heaven; I want to go soon and be with Jesus. I give up all to him, and let him do as he likes with me."— He asked Mr. S. to pray for and with him, and to tell Jesus that he wanted to go to him. Mr. S. talked and prayed with him probably for the last time, as we have no expectation of his living till morning."

After Scovell had partaken, this afternoon, of some ice cream, which his father procured for him, and which was very grateful to his taste, he said to his mother, "God has answered every prayer I have prayed since I became sick. I prayed him not to let me suffer a great deal and to help me to bear it patiently, and now, when I wanted some ice cream, I prayed for it, and God let me have it." Soon after, when he was vomiting almost constantly, he said, "Mamma, you said it would hurt me to vomit, but it does n't. I prayed God not to let it."

At 8 : 45 P. M., the doctor came and expressed the opinion that Scovell might possibly live two days yet. His apparent chances for twenty-four hours' life were better to-night than they were last night, but he spoke only from symptoms that might change at any moment, and he could give no encouragement for more than a few hours' continuance. Conversation during the night was avoided, that the child's strength might not be unnecessarily wasted.

Saturday morning found him still living, and very clear in mind, but much reduced, and for the first time he complained of a difficulty to speak. At eight o'clock, seeing his mother near him, he said, " I want to go to heaven ; I don't want to stay here any longer." At 8 : 45, he roused up, and noticing a lady present who had called to sit awhile by his bedside, he said, " I thank you for coming to help my mamma." Soon after, he said, " I want to die ;" and then, noticing that the expression drew tears from the eyes of his mother, he added, addressing her, " I don't want you or father to cry."—

At about 9 : 15, Dr. Cross called and discovered a slight reäction, causing warm hands, but the pulse was more uneven. He thought he might live twenty-four hours longer, but said he was liable to sink away at any time. At 9 : 40 his grandfather came in to see him. He aroused and said, "I want to be quiet grandpa; I will give you a kiss if you want it." At ten o'clock, Mr. Samson again called and had a brief interview with him. He said, "Mr. Samson, I am going to heaven, and I want Jesus to hurry and take me." Mr. S. asked him if he was not willing to wait God's time; to which he replied, "Yes, but I would rather Jesus would hurry." He expressed great anxiety that his dear mother should have strength given her to bear the affliction that was about to come upon her. He said, "I pray the Lord continually to make my mother willing to let me go, and I want you to pray for her too." Soon after, as his father sat by his bedside weeping, he said, "Don't cry, father!"— Upon receiving the reply that his father could not always control his feelings, and that it was hard to part with his dear boy, he said, "*But I am going to heaven!*" evidently feeling that that fact should dry up all tears. In reply to his father's questioning, he said, "I have thought sometimes that you spoke too harshly to me, or punished or scolded me too hastily and when I did not really deserve it, but I knew your mind was perplexed with your business, and I prayed God that you might quickly get over your feelings, and that he would not let me get angry." And then he added, "*Father, I have thought at times that I was a Christian for a long while.*" He seemed to have been in doubt only because he did not know just what emotions to expect with a change of heart. It was evident that his hope was not first obtained on his death-bed, but that strength and a clear faith, and dying grace were given him of the Spirit to meet the last change.

At 11:45 some friends from Suspension Bridge called. He saw them for a moment and bid them good-by. Then a clerk in his uncle's store, to whom he was much attached, came in. Scovell bade him good-by and said, " I am going to die, Leonard ; and I am going to heaven ; kiss me."   At one o'clock, his grandfather being in, for the first time it was noticed that conversation in the room disturbed him. From the note book before referred to, the following extract is taken :

" He talks only when spoken to, or when he wants something, and then with as few words as possible. This is a great change since yesterday at this hour. Oh, with what agony of heart we watch every new indication of waning vitality ! Lord help us, his parents, to give him up, even as he has given himself up to Jesus. Give us strength and faith to surrender back this precious gift to the all-wise Giver, and to say from the heart, ' Not as I will, but as thou wilt'—' Thy will be done !' "

At 3 : 20, Scovell called his father and mother. He wanted to see them together again. He said he was happy, but he did not want to converse with them. At about four o'clock, information was received by telegraph that Scovell's grandfather McCol-

17

lum would arrive by the next train. An hour after, he came, and the unexpected meeting was one of touching interest. The grey hairs of the patriarch of nearly three score years and ten fell over the face of the dying child, as he stooped to take the last kiss of affection from his only grandson; and deep was his emotion as he received the same clear evidence that had been given to others, that the bed of the sufferer was soon to be exchanged for a seat among the angels at the right hand of the blessed Saviour, in that holy city, where "there shall be no more death, neither sorrow nor crying, neither shall there be any more pain;" and where "the inhabitants shall not say I am sick."— The interview was necessarily short, and at its conclusion, Scovell inquired how long before Mr. Riggs would come. Upon being told, he expressed a strong anxiety to live to see him, and occasionally he repeated the inquiry as to when he would arrive. At seven Mr. Samson called, but Scovell was too weak for conversation. He exhibited his usual gratitude for his kindness, and listened

with attention to the prayer that was offered—the last he ever heard from the lips of
this most faithful friend.

In the evening, in accordance with Scovell's desire, his father telegraphed to Mr.
Marshall, at Syracuse, these solemn words:
"Give Scovell's dying message to Sabbath
school, ' Be Christians ; meet me in heaven.' "
He added, in speaking to his parents and
friends, the injunction: "Tell all my mates
to love the Lord, and lay themselves at
Jesus' feet." He had no anxiety for himself,
for he felt that his feet were planted upon
the "Rock of Ages;" but, as his moments
became fewer and his breath shorter; as his
eyes were about closing to the sights of earth
to open upon the splendors which surround
the throne of God, his desire increased that
they who had been his companions in school
and play might hereafter be permitted to
walk with him the golden streets of the New
Jerusalem.

At 11 : 30 at night, Mr. Riggs arrived, and
upon being informed of the fact, the child
expressed great desire to see him without

delay. "Have him come up immediately, have him come up immediately," he exclaimed, and when his father. asked if he should not wait a few moments, until his attendant could make some changes about his bed, he replied, "No! I want to see him immediately." The meeting of the devoted minister and the dying boy was deeply solemn and affecting. Rallying all his energies, Scovell drew his arm from the bed, placed his hand in that of his friend, and said, "So you have come, have you?" And then, after a moment's pause for strength, he proceeded to exhibit the fruits of his former instruction, and to give his dying testimony of his faith in God through Jesus Christ. The effort soon exhausted him, and he quickly fell asleep. After this, he conversed but little with any one. His strength was rapidly wasting, and the difficulty of speech increased. His sleep was more disturbed, and he was more restless, whether awake or asleep. At six o'clock on Sunday morning, Mr. Riggs again came in the room, and at Scovell's request sat by the bedside in such a position that the dying boy could look at his parents and his dear friend together, and commune with them by sight when failing strength would not permit him to take part in conversation. He had often desired his parents to take that position, so that he could give expression with his eyes to that glowing love which seemed to grow brighter and increase as he approached the river of death, and caught glimpses, with his mortal vision, of the " shining shore " beyond. Sometimes he would take hold of a hand of each of his parents, and tenderly say to them, " When I am gone, you will love each other *always* for my sake, wo n't you ? "

At nine o'clock, it was evident that Scovell was very near his end, that the ardent desire of his heart that Jesus would hurry and take him to himself was soon to be gratified. Friends gathered around his bed to witness his departure. His mind remained clear and his faith bright, and with occasional ejaculatory expressions, he continued to give evidence of his firm trust in God. He called for Mr. Samson and Mr. Riggs, and they were sent

17*

for. When they came together into the room, instead of the usual salutation with which he was accustomed to greet his friends, he simply said " Good-by Mr. Samson ; good-by Mr. Riggs." He was fully conscious that he was dying, and wanted his friends around him that they might witness his departure. About three quarters of an hour before he ceased to breath, he called all those in the room by name, and bade each of them good-by. He asked his father to kiss him, and after he had done it, he said, " Kiss me again, papa." When his little feet were treading the very verge of Jordan, and prayer was being offered by Mr. Riggs, at the mention of " Our Saviour," he exclaimed, " Yes! Yes! He is all I have now ; he is all I love." His Sabbath and day schools, and his superintendent and teacher, whom he had loved so much, were in his mind to the very last, and Mr. Marshall's name was twice uttered during the last ten minutes of his life. He was much distressed by thirst during the last three days of his sickness, and called almost continually for water. When very near his end, his eyes earnestly gazing toward heaven, he constantly exclaimed, "Water, water, clear water; water, clear water." And when he wanted to drink he would drop his eyes and add, "Water, please." Then again he would turn them heavenward and continue to exclaim, "Water, water; clear water," etc. Was he permitted to catch glimpses by faith of that fountain of living waters of which he so earnestly longed to drink? The last words he uttered were, "I shall soon drink clear water in heaven." A few minutes after, at twenty minutes past eleven o'clock, A. M., his spirit passed peacefully away to God who gave it.

Scovell's attending physician, Dr. Cross, in a letter written some time after the death, said he could remember "but little of the treatment that was peculiar in the case, but of moral and religious impressions I do recollect much. His patience under the most acute sufferings; his strong, natural and active mind; his deep knowledge of religious truths; his faith in the justice of God and trust in the merits of a merciful Redeemer, were all too remarkable not to leave their impression on every one who witnessed them as I did."

The consulting physician, Dr. Augustus Jukes, was the last to give up the hope of saving the life of the dear boy, and through all his attendance upon him, evinced an uncommon sympathy with anxious and sorrowing parents and friends. In subsequent conversations, he has said that he never felt such emotions in his heart as when he first saw Scovell, suffering, but patient, happy and resigned, upon his death bed. Such perfect development, mental and physical, he had scarce ever seen, and he felt that if there was any thing in the power of man that could save his life, it must be done. To him it had been a great mystery, that a being made with such faculties for usefulness in this world as it was evident that Scovell possessed, should have been removed so early from it. "But," said he, "now we see through a glass darkly, but it will all be made plain to us." In a letter subsequently written to Scovell's parents, he adds, "I am sure that time and reflection will convince you that He that ruleth all things well has done this also in love."

During his last sickness, Scovell exhibited the most remarkable patience and resignation, constantly studying to relieve his friends from trouble and care. He would often say to his mother, "Ain't I good, mamma? Ain't I patient? I pray God to make me good and patient." His gratitude for attention to his wants and efforts to relieve his sufferings, continued till almost his last breath. Mr. Samson remarked that he never talked and prayed with him, but that as he bade him good-by, the little sufferer thanked him for calling, for his words of comfort, and for his sympathy. Seldom, through his whole sickness, was any thing done for him without his giving verbal evidence of his appreciation of the kindness; and for the last drink of water he took from the hand of his nurse — one who had been in the family from his early infancy, and to whom he was tenderly attached — he looked up in her face affectionately and uttered a simple, heart-felt "thank you." They were the last words he addressed to her. His wants in this world were ended, and he was about going to drink from the fountain of living waters which flow out from the throne of God.

CHAPTER X.

St. Catharines after Death.

19 "No thorn is hidden to wound me there;
    There's nothing of chill or blight,
    Or sighing to blend with the balmy air,—
    No sorrow,—no pain,—no night!"

20 "No *parting?*" I asked, in a burst of joy:
    And the lovely illusion broke;
    My rapture had banished my beautiful boy,—
    To a shadowy void I spoke!

CHAPTER X.

Rev. Mr. Riggs, in writing subsequently of these solemn death-bed scenes, said:

"I have stood by many death beds. I have watched the departure from earth of many who are now, no doubt, in the heavenly city. But never have I stood where heaven seemed to come nearer to earth than at the death bed of this loved boy. His life had prepared me to hope great things for him, but even my intimate knowledge of that life did not secure me against surprise at the strength of his faith and the triumph of his confidence. His hope in Christ was scarcely shaken by one wave of fear. His was the trust of the child in an almighty Father. He was beyond the necessity of instruction in the essential points of Christian

18

faith. His simple, yet comprehensive statements of the plan of salvation, not only evinced his extraordinary knowledge of the Gospel, but put to the blush many of the studied abstractions of the schools. Christ and his salvation were living realities to him. Conscious of his need, he bound them to his heart with all the earnestness of child-like belief. God had spoken; he believed! Oh! the beautiful simplicity of the Gospel of Christ! Never shall I forget the preaching of this dear boy to my own soul on this theme as I stood beside his bed of triumph!

In recalling the scenes of those last hours, I have been greatly impressed with the fact that Scovell's spiritual experience was not, as is frequently the case, a *spasmodic thing.* He never needed to be recalled to it from other thoughts. Its deep undercurrent flowed constantly on. Every topic was brought into its sweep. The bright light of the sun, the kindness of friends, the love of parents, even his clothing and his medicines, all seemed to be spiritualized by him. The cool water which refreshed his fevered frame suggested to his mind the crystal fountains which gush forth from the throne of God, and of whose waters the redeemed ones drink. '*I shall soon drink clear water in heaven*,' were the last words which he uttered to his earthly friends. His whole being was set towards God and heaven, and nothing could recall his spirit from its chosen direction. Would that we all, in life as well as in death, were the followers of this honored boy."

From a letter recently received by Scovell's parents, from Mr. Samson, the following extracts are taken :

"When we heard of Scovell's sickness, it brought sorrow to our hearts. Nothing but consulting his good with reference to his illness could have kept Mrs. S. and myself from his bedside. And when once, as you doubtless recollect, I did, for a moment, meet him there, I felt that I could not leave him until I knew his heart. He was lying with his face to the wall, but turned partly over to speak to me. He was in great suffering, and immediately resumed the position in which I found him. I at once opened to him the subject of religion, and the instant he heard the name of Christ he seemed to forget his pains and turned again toward me, that he might the more easily listen to what I was saying. Just then the physician entered, and I retired without receiving any verbal expression of your child's feelings. But, if I had never seen him again, with the recollection of the promptness with which he turned towards me, and the indescribable expression which lighted up his countenance as I spoke to him of Jesus and heaven, I could never have entertained a single doubt as to his full preparation for the future world.

At a later date a message came to our door, saying that Scovell desired to see me.— Gladly did I obey that summons, and never, no never, shall I forget that look as his eye caught mine, nor that voice as the first words fell from his lips: 'Mr. Samson, I want to be an angel, and I want you to pray that I may be an angel.' It has often been my privilege to stand by the dying Christian, (favored place,) but never before did I seem to be so near the gate of heaven; and when your Scovell went through, it did seem to me it would be a great privilege could we all go with him. My repeated visits to his death bed exhibited to me more of the power of religion on the heart than I ever expected to see on earth. Upon those scenes I love to dwell. I love to think how a lad of eleven years could let go of earth, and how he could pant to be an angel and to be with Jesus.— My earliest impressions on visiting Scovell's bedside were that his ·sickness was unto death. No one could doubt for one moment but that his sufferings were extreme, and yet a smile constantly played on his countenance. Not one complaining word did I ever hear from him, and it seemed to be his constant fear that some one would suffer on his account.   *   *   *   *

These are but a few of the breathings of your Scovell's heart which fell from his lips as I visited him from time to time. And then, as he laid his little hand in mine at parting, a gentle 'thank you' was uttered, which one could see came from the heart.—

18*

Yes, no one could stand by his bedside and see and hear him, but would feel that it was heart work with him, yea, God's work in the heart. I never stood there for one moment but I felt covered with shame that I, an old professor, was but a babe of yesterday in spiritual things, when by the side of this boy of eleven years. And, how peacefully your darling went home! There was no struggle, no groan, not even a scowl, but a sweet, a heavenly smile was playing upon his every feature. We had seen your son panting to be with Jesus, and how gently was he folded in his Saviour's arms.

And now, dear brother, dear sister, would you have it otherwise? Would you have your son an inhabitant of that heavenly land where the leaves of the trees are for the healing of the nations; where no sorrow nor sighing can ever enter? Or would you bring him back to this sin-stricken world, where we all rather sigh than live? Would you even take him from the embraces of Jesus that you might again fold him in your paternal arms? Does it cause sorrow to fill your hearts that your Scovell has left you? Should it not cause joy too, that he has gone to that home for which his soul so ardently longed? Are you not in danger of feeling that there is seldom sorrow like unto your sorrow? But is there often joy like unto your joy? Many a parent has been called to drink to the very dregs the same cup of sorrow of which you have drank, but without its being mingled with that sweetness which has led others to doubt whether it could, on the whole, have been bitter to you. Many of us have been allowed the assurance that our departed ones were in heaven, but few, like you, have been permitted to stand with them on the threshold, and as the gates were opened for their admission, to hear notes almost divine. My dear friends, if we, like Scovell, will lay ourselves at Jesus' feet, willing that he should do by us just what he has a mind to, Scovell's joys will be our joys, and we shall yet enjoy with him that 'rest for the weary' of which he so delighted to think and sing."

Scovell's body, clothed for the grave in the same suit that he wore to church on the Sabbath morning previous to his sickness, was laid in a beautiful black walnut coffin, lined and cushioned with satin, with a satin pillow, and upon the cover was a silver plate, upon which was neatly engraved the following words: "SCOVELL HAYNES McCOLLUM.— Died September 16th, 1860. Aged 11 years and 4 months." Beautiful white lillies were in his hands and upon his pillow; and the hand of affection entwined an elegant wreath of white flowers which encircled the plate upon his coffin lid, and was let down upon it into the grave. His countenance retained a life-like expression, peaceful and lovely, and his body, as it lay robed for sepulture, appeared like one in a natural sleep rather than in the repose of death. Upon the marble mantle in each parlor stood a photographic likeness of the departed child, the frame encircled with a wreath of myrtle, and on either side were vases of Parian marble holding beautiful boquets of white flowers, intermingled with sprigs of green. Similar vases and boquets were placed in other rooms in the house.

The funeral was attended at 3 o'clock, P. M., on Monday, September 17th, at the residence of D. P. Haynes, Esq., grandfather of the deceased, in St. Catharines, and a large company assembled to condole with the bereaved ones, and pay the last tribute of respect to a child whom they had dearly loved.

Rev. Mr. Riggs opened the exercises by reading the first and twenty-third Psalms of David, portions of scripture so precious to Scovell when living, and particularly during his last sickness. Brief addresses were made by Rev. G. M. W. Carey, pastor of the Queen Street Baptist Church, at St. Catharines, and by Rev. William C. Wisner, D. D., pastor of the first Presbyterian Church at Lockport, N. Y. Prayer was offered by Rev. Joshua Cook, of Lewiston; Scovell's favorite Sabbath school hymn, " Rest for the Weary " was sung, and then the body was borne to the cemetery, followed by the afflicted relatives and sympathizing friends.—

At the grave, after the hymn "Thou art gone to the grave" had been sung, Rev. Mr. Riggs thanked the friends, in behalf of the family, for their sympathy and kindly attention, and then made an appropriate address, in which among other things, he remarked that, though for the last few days, he had wept in sympathy with bereaved parents and friends, though he had wept because of a personal loss in this death, he was conscious that his was now a different experience.— He shared the feelings of a conqueror rather than a mourner. His thoughts ran out upon a triumph. In yonder upper room there had been witnessed a conflict. The "King of Terrors" had there been met by this tender youth. Young and feeble as he was, he had been summoned to the encounter with the last great enemy. And what had been the the result? Death had obtained a partial victory. The body had surrendered to his power, and was now still and cold in his narrow prison. "Yes! this sad trophy of death is here before us. Thus much of victory we celebrate over this open grave. In a nobler

sense this feeble youth was the conqueror of
death.   The shield of Christian faith pro-
tected his soul from every arrow of fear
which was shot against him.   The strength
of his victorious Saviour nerved his frail
arm.   And with the triumphant shout, ' Oh
death, where is thy sting? Oh grave, where
is thy victory?' his rejoicing spirit went up
from that battle field to endless life.   Angels
came down to the shining gates to welcome
the little conqueror.   The companies of the
redeemed crowded his triumphal way.—
Christ himself arose to meet his victorious
soldier, and to place on his head the crown
of unfading glory.   What wonder, therefore,
if we are full of joy! We do but repeat the
song which has already rung through heaven, when we fill our hearts with rejoicing
over this event.   And when we think of his
triumph, and his heavenly welcome, and his
happy state before the throne, we cannot
wish him back. Even these weeping parents,
much as they loved their boy, and much
as they must miss him—would not bid him
return. They could not find it in their hearts

to take that crown from his head, that robe from his spirit form, that harp from his hand, that new song from his happy, sinless heart, and bring him back to this world of sin and strife and sorrow. We know that they rejoice with us over his conquest and his rest. May we all so think of this triumph and of its lessons to us, that the friends we leave behind may rejoice over our death as a victory."

At the conclusion of his remarks, which are here in part reported, Rev. Mr. Riggs offered prayer, and then the mourners turned with solemn sadness from a spot that will be ever sacred to them as the resting place of the earthly remains of the departed child.

Rev. Mr. Carey and Rev. Dr. Wisner were requested to write out for publication the substance of their remarks, but instead thereof sent the following letters :

LETTER FROM REV. MR. CAREY.

"St. Catharines, Oct. 15, 1860.

My Dear Sir :—It is with mingled sorrow and joy, that I yield to your request, to send you some of my recollections of your late only and beloved son, Scovell Haynes Mc-Collum. I was acquainted with Scovell for over four years. To me he was a boy of great promise. I took an unusual interest in him. I never knew a boy of Scovell's years to have a character so mature as he. His thoughts and expressions were so rare and original, that I always heard him with pleasure, and talked with him as if he were my equal in years and experience. Where-ever I met him I was glad to see him, and he always appeared glad to see me.

His bounding footstep, his joyous look, his beaming eye, his open countenance, and his frank salutation, were exceedingly pleasant to me. Now that he is gone, I remember these things, for small and trivial as they may appear, they contributed to form the grand total of his lovely character.

In an intellectual, moral, and religious point of view, Scovell was a remarkable boy. His anxiety for education, the development of his intellect under scholastic training and discipline, the progress that he made in his

19

studies, were to me truly astonishing in a boy of his years. His willingness to forego pleasure and recreation to enter upon and resume his studies; the apparent ease with which he made the sacrifice, indicated his strong desire and inherent taste for mental culture and development.

In his morals he was scrupulously exact. Richly did he repay the care and pains of pious parents, and grand parents, and teachers. During the four years of my acquaintance with him, I never heard an improper word escape his lips. His distinctions between right and wrong were marked, and his moral sense lively and strong.

His religious convictions and faith were unusually deep and mature. Truly he was taught of the *Spirit*. Out of the mouth of a child God has perfected praise. From the heart and lips of a boy God has elicited a testimony to the truth as it is in Jesus, which has rarely been equaled, and seldom surpassed by those of maturer years. I shall never forget the attention he paid to a discourse that I preached a few weeks before his death, which, I believe, was the last discourse he heard. The text was taken from Luke 9 : 26. ' For whosoever shall be ashamed of me and of my words, of him shall the Son of Man be ashamed, when he shall come in his own glory, and in his Father's, and of the holy angels.' As I spoke of what it is to be ashamed of Christ, how absurd it is, and how awful are the consequences, he never moved in his seat, and never, during the discourse, withdrew his steady gaze from my countenance. As he sat in a direct line before me I could not but perceive his marked attention. I have since understood that on his return to his grandfather's, where he was then visiting, that he spoke of the discourse, and seemed much affected by the truths he had heard. Assuredly Scovell was not ashamed of Christ. To old and young, during his sickness and on his death-bed, did he speak of Jesus.— His ministry was short, but earnest, and impressive ; and may we not hope efficient in doing much good? Eternity alone can disclose the blessed results of his witnessing for Christ. The faith of mature Christians was strengthened by his testimony for Christ; and those who had not given themselves to Jesus, were aroused and deeply moved by his earnest appeals. I saw him, for the last time, on the second day previous to his death. I inquired of him, ' Scovell, are you happy?' ' Happy,' said he with a beaming countenance, ' I am going to drink of the River of of Life, and I shall never thirst again.' After a short pause he added, ' Pray for me, that Jesus may be with me till I die; and when I die, that I may go to be with Jesus.' I knelt and offered a short prayer with him, and bade him farewell, till we meet again in heaven.

My dear sir, may the God of all grace and consolation comfort you and your worthy wife for the loss of such a child. Did I say *loss?* Should I not say *gain?* What a gain! to have such a child to give to God, not only to his service on earth, but also to his enjoyment in heaven. Happy parents! Happy grand parents! Happy friends! for such a boy. Worthy indeed of being classed with the pious youth of Bible story—with the Samuels and Timothys of the Old and New Dispensations. Dry your tears and rejoice; Jesus has taken your darling boy, as the sun draws up the dew-drops, to be bathed in glory, and to rest on his bosom.

> Farewell, dear boy, one day we hope to meet thee,
>   Beyond the reach of death, disease, and pain;
> In pastures green, by waters still we'll greet thee,
>   Led by thy Lord the Lamb, along the flowery plain.
> Farewell, e'en now what glories on thee rise,
>   In thy Father's house, in the celestial Paradise.

G. M. W. CAREY,
Pastor of Queen St. Bap. Ch., St. Catharines, C. W."

LETTER FROM REV. WM. C. WISNER, D.D.

"LOCKPORT, N. Y., Oct. 11th, 1860.

MY DEAR FRIEND:—I have received your kind letter, requesting for publication the remarks I made at the funeral of our much loved Scovell. I cannot reproduce them, nor is it best that I should attempt it. They were entirely extemporaneous, and were delivered under circumstances so sad, and a

19*

pressure of feeling so deep, that I do not now recollect even the line of remark I pursued. I loved Scovell far more than I was aware until he came to be translated to his home in heaven. Every sentence I uttered proceeded from a bleeding heart. I can truly say that, within the entire circle of my acquaintance, I know of no child of his age of equal maturity and promise. He possessed a personal appearance unusually attractive, and a manliness of deportment altogether beyond his years; and his intellectual and moral developments were truly remarkable. That his heart was given up to God, and his life consecrated to his service, we cannot doubt. How sadly delightful were the scenes of his death bed! What a triumph of faith in the death of a mere child! Surely we cannot shed a tear for him, though we do and must weep for ourselves.

I think of you continually in your loneliness, and the thought is constantly present with me, that if the death of the dear child is such an affliction to me, it must be well-nigh overwhelming to his parents. But, my

dear afflicted brother, there is seldom a death
with so much to comfort. The cloud is a
dark one, but it is spanned, from end to end,
with a most beautiful bow of promise. You
cannot view Scovell as dead but as glorified.
I can hear his sweet voice, full of the melody
of heaven, calling out to you from some
celestial embattlement,

> ' Come this way, father;
> Steer straight for me :
> Here, safe in heaven,
> I am waiting for thee.'

And there he will wait, in bliss the most
perfect, until he shall welcome his father and
mother within those pearly gates, and clasp
them each in their turn to his young heart.
I have no doubt but that you will see and
know Scovell in heaven, and that the meeting
will be one of great joy. I dare not write all
I believe and feel on the subject, lest I should
appear too enthusiastic. Eye hath not seen,
nor has imagination conceived what is in re-
serve for us at our reünion in heaven.
    I have been greatly affected by the deep

and universal sensation which has been produced among the large circle of your friends,
by the death of your child. If heart-felt and
wide sympathy is a solace to you, (and surely
it must be,) you have it poured into your.
wounded heart from every quarter. Your
deep sorrow, and the virtues of your loved
boy, have been made the sad theme of soul-
stirring song, and of the most touching eloquence. Your friends, besides showing a deep
sympathy, have exhibited a personal grief
which certainly must afford a balm to your
wounded and desolate spirits. You have
every consolation that can be possibly afforded under so sad a bereavement. Not any
thing that you could desire in connection
with it has been withheld. All that remains
for us is sweetly to bow to the will of our
heavenly Father, and improve spiritually
the sad providence. The Lord gave and the
Lord hath taken away, and blessed be his
great and holy name. Even so Father, for
so it seemeth good in thy sight. Not my
will, but thine, oh God, be done. These light
afflictions, which are for a moment, work

out for us a far more exceeding and eternal
weight of glory.

This letter, although addressed to yourself,
is intended equally for your excellent lady.
It is wonderful indeed, how by the grace of
God, she has been sustained under so severe
an affliction.   *   .   *   *

I am, my dear brother, as ever, your affectionate and sympathizing friend,

WM. C. WISNER."

For nearly a quarter of a century, Dr.
Wisner has been a warmly attached friend
of the family of Scovell's father, and for
many years their pastor.   In his remarks
at the funeral, he alluded in a very feeling
manner to this fact, speaking of his having
laid hands upon the child now deceased in
the ordinance of baptism, and to the pleasure
he had enjoyed with him during a recent
visit to his father's house.   He also referred
most touchingly to the child's now sainted
grandmother, (McCollum) who had watched
his growing years from her heavenly home,
and whose spirit had, no doubt, hovered

around his death bed, and been the first to welcome him within the pearly gates of the new Jerusalem. Oh, what a blessed privilege here to anticipate such heavenly reunions; but how much more blessed must be the reality!

During the week of the funeral, Scovell's parents remained at St. Catharines, and received evidences of warmest sympathy from their friends and the friends of their departed child. Numerous letters were received, all overflowing with expressions of consolation and comfort. The following, written by persons who had known Scovell intimately as a pupil, are selected for publication. Miss Linsley was his "drawing" teacher, as stated elsewhere, and accompanying her letter was a beautiful little sketch of the falls of Minnehaha, in Minnesota. Mr. Marshall is the teacher of the day school, and superintendent of the Sabbath school with which Scovell was connected at the time of his death.

LETTER FROM MISS EMMA A. LINSLEY.

"St. Catharines, C. W., Sept. 20, 1860.

My Dear Mrs. McCollum:—Here is a bit of penciling that I drew for Scovell, mostly last Thursday. During last week I learned, at different times, that he was better, and I was not aware that he was worse that day. I had thought that, perhaps, this scratch might amuse him for a moment, on his sick bed, for, when well, he had asked me to sketch a trifle for him. But the next news I received from your darling was that he was failing fast, and could not live long. I need not, I cannot express to you my feelings then.

Allow me to say that your Scovell, when with me, was a favorite with all my pupils, who knew him. He was so noble and conscientious, so kind and affectionate at all times. In all sincerity, I too would say, with the Rev. Dr. Wisner, 'I never saw so mature a mind in one so young.' I cannot but recall to mind how, a few days before he left us, he had fondly anticipated returning to his studies, under his beloved teacher in Syracuse. But God saw fit to place him in a school infinitely higher, where his Jesus is his teacher, and angels and just men made perfect are his companions. Oh! I know you rejoice that he is on high, though you and your dear husband and parents will see him no more here below. And I think I hear you say, in the language of another:

> 'Yet firm my foot, for well I know
>   The goal cannot be far,
> And over, through the rifted clouds,
>   Shines out one steady star:
> For when my son went up, he left
>   The pearly gates ajar!'

Affectionately yours,

EMMA A. LINSLEY."

LETTER FROM MR. JAMES MARSHALL.

"SYRACUSE, Sept. 15, 1860.

MY DEAR FRIEND:—Your dispatch containing 'Scovell's dying message' to the Sunday school has just arrived. Is it possible

that Scovell is dead?* Scovell's dying message! Is that intelligent, that beautiful, that
noble boy gone? How anxiously have I
been waiting for his return to the school
room! He was so courteous, so obedient,
so kind and friendly to me *always*, that I
have thought of him often in my summer's
vacation, and impatiently waited since school
began, to hear his friendly morning greeting.
But he is dead, dead! No more shall we
meet him on earth. No more shall his min-
glings in our circles and recitations give us
glimpses of future promise and usefulness.
But ' death loves a shining mark.' Strange,
strange are the ways of Providence. Frowns
seem resting every where. Death and
mourning must humble and warn us. But
oh, how beautiful is that faith that sees a
smiling face behind a frowning Providence,
a faith that never falters in the truth that
our Father ' doeth all things well.' I have
only time to send Mrs. McCollum and your-

---

*Scovell's dying message was sent on Saturday after-
noon, and the impression was erroneously conveyed that
he was then dead.

20

self my sympathy, and the sympathy of
many, many friends that have watched that
boy with interest. But how weak, how
powerless is all human sympathy in the hour
of death. Only in the shadow of the Cross
is there comfort—is there peace to the bleeding heart. Only in Christ is there rest to the
soul when weary watching over the death
bed of an only child—a noble and promising
boy. In Christ alone is there strength to
sustain the soul in such great afflictions.—
Scovell dead! I cannot realize it. I felt
proud of my pupil, so full of promise. He
was a boy of uncommon talents. Strangers
remarked it when they heard his original
declamation at the close of school last term,
on 'Knowledge is Power.' We shall miss
him from our day school, for he was a favorite. We shall miss him from our Sunday
school, for he was always prompt and prepared with thoughtful inquiry. I shall deliver his last words with sadness mingled with
joy: with sadness because he is gone from
our midst forever—with joy, because he has
gone, rejoicing in the Christian's hope, trust-

ing to a Saviour's love, and leaving us his prayer to meet him in heaven. I hope his message may arrest the souls of his class and direct their thoughts to Christ. 'Be Christians—meet me in heaven.' What a rich—what a beautiful legacy to his associates!—May it be stamped upon the minds of us all. May the voice of the Spirit ever whisper it to our souls. 'Be Christians—meet me in heaven.' But, my friend, I can only give you my deep sympathy in your great, great loss, and point you for comfort to the Fountain of all joy and peace—who giveth and taketh away. Let us ever give God the praise. Most affectionately,

JAMES MARSHALL."

On Sabbath afternoon, September 23rd, the First Presbyterian Church, at St. Catharines, was crowded by sympathizing friends, to listen to a funeral sermon by Rev. Mr. Riggs. The sixth and seventh verses of the first chapter of Jeremiah were selected as a text, as follows:

"Then said I, ah, Lord God! behold I cannot speak for I am a child.

"But the Lord said unto me, say not I am a child: for thou shalt go to all that I shall send thee, and whatsoever I command thee thou shalt speak."

After a brief introduction the speaker said:

"The sore affliction which has called us together to-day, affords a fresh illustration of the truth thus suggested by the text. As the youth of Jeremiah, and his conscious weakness, were no hindrance to the bestowment of his large commission, nor to his faithful fulfillment of it, so the youth of him whose loss we here mourn did not prevent his call to a large work, and a most impressive message. The dear boy whom God has taken from us, had the call been made to him in form, as it was made to the young prophet, would doubtless have replied with him, 'Ah, Lord God! behold I cannot speak for I am a child!' Yet God has in reality called him to a most important and responsible ministry. From his sick-bed pulpit, he has been commissioned to proclaim the

Gospel of Christ with a power seldom equaled.   God himself has spoken through the
dying boy.   The youthful child has become
a preacher.

In the name of this young preacher, and
under the commission of his dying request,
I stand before you to-day, to give simple utterance to the lessons which his ministry sug-
gests.   'He being dead yet speaketh.'"

He then proceeded to speak of the different lessons to be drawn from the life and
death of this "boy preacher," alluded to the
character of the deceased, in language which
has before been quoted, and concluded the
discourse as follows:

"As we close our public meditation upon
this young preacher's message, let us gather
up its leading truths into a practical application to our hearts.   God has commissioned
him to speak to us of our immortal existence
after death ;—of the essential oneness of our
present and our future life ;—of the preparation which we, as sinners, need to make for
death and for eternity ;—and of the only
true standard of value and of length of life,

20*

as found in our worthy employment of it, as immortal beings. I should not be true to you, my dear hearers, nor to the dying request of him for whom I speak to-day, did I not ask you *how you stand related to these solemn truths.* Do you realize that they are truths? Have they impressed your heart and influenced your life? Nay, turn not thoughtlessly away from this questioning, as you have so often done before. God is speaking to you to-day in the death of this dear boy. He has often spoken to you before of these things. Oh! why have you compelled him to speak to you yet again in this new grief? How many loved ones must yet be sacrificed to your sinful stupidity? How many mourners must yet weep over departed friends, before you will begin to live wisely for eternity? Oh! trifle not, I beseech you, with these messages from God! Turn not to-day from the voice which speaks to you from the coming world! The truths which it utters are eternal realities. You must soon meet them. Life is short. 'There is but a step between you and death!' Before another Sabbath

dawns, weeping friends, all hopeless in their
grief, may gather around your grave. ' *This
very night* your soul may be required of you.'
Shall it be that, in spite of a Saviour's entreaty and blood—in spite of all the faithful
admonitions of the past—in spite of the
warnings of this death—you will live on re-
gardless of your immortality, and with nc
anxiety whether life or death shall be your
portion throughout eternity ? Ah, impenitent
man ! what if your next warning should be
the knocking of death at the door of your
own life, and the touch of his cold hand upon
your own heart.

Dear children of the Sabbath school, let
me speak a word to yon. Scovell is dead.
That bright boy, who Sabbath after Sabbath
sat down with you to study the Word of
God, and whom you all loved so well to
meet, will never come with you again to the
Sabbath school on earth. God has sent for
him to go home. We have laid his little
body in the grave, where it will sleep safely
till the morning of the resurrection day.
Angels watch over it now. And his spirit,

that which made his eye so bright, and his thought so quick, and his heart so loving, has gone up to heaven. We could not see it go. We did not see his Saviour, when he came down into that little sick room and took the soul of our dear friend away with him. We could not follow with our sight the shining path along which they journeyed. We could not see the gates of pearl swing open to receive them into the shining city. Yet we are sure that Scovell has gone to be with Christ forever in heaven. We are sure of this, because he loved Christ. And you remember the promise of Christ, 'He that loveth me shall be loved of my father, and I will love him, and manifest myself to him.' Yes! he has gone where there is 'rest for the weary;' where the 'clear water' of the river of life, of which he has so longed to drink, gushes from the throne of God; where the week is all Sabbath; and where Jesus gathers about him his own Sabbath school class. I seem even now to see Scovell amid that happy throng of children as they crowd around their Saviour, to hear the pleasant words which fall from his lips. There they stand, robed in the white of Heaven, with shining crowns upon their heads, and harps of gold in their hands. And hark! do you not hear that unearthly music? It is the melody of those happy children, singing the new songs of Heaven before the throne. 'Happy songsters! when shall we your chorus join!'

Dear children, I have an invitation for you to join that school and that song. Christ has invited you, for he has said, 'Suffer little children to come unto me!' And Scovell has invited you too. This is the dying message which he wished me to deliver to you for him: 'BE CHRISTIANS; MEET ME IN HEAVEN!' 'Tell all my mates to *love the Lord, and lay themselves at Jesus' feet!*' Think of this, dear children. Christ wants you to come to Him. And Scovell wants you to '*be Christians, and meet him in Heaven.*' Try to hear his earnest voice as he invites you thus, and as he tells you how you may get to Heaven. '*Lay yourselves at Jesus' feet!*' But some of you will think,

'*By and by I will do this.   Before I die I will love the Lord, but not just now.*'   If one of you is thinking so, I have another message to you from your young friend.   Before he died, he asked of one who came to bid him farewell, 'Are you ready to die *now?*'   He replied, 'I am afraid not.'   'Then,' said the dying boy, ' you must give your heart to Jesus now.   *Now is the time!   Now is the time!*'   Oh! remember this warning!   It will not do to delay.   '*Love God*' now! '*Lay yourselves at Jesus' feet*' this very day! Then you will be sure to meet Scovell in Heaven when you die.

As I turn to you, dear friends, whose hearts this affliction most nearly touches, I feel that my mission has been entirely anticipated.   There is no need that I should speak to you.   I would tell you of God's sovereignty as relieved by the thought that He is your careful and loving Father.   I would speak to you of willing and cheerful resignation to His will.   I would speak of consolation in your God. I would urge to faith which clings to the promises, and to hope which triumphs over sorrow. But of all these your dying boy has already spoken. He has opened before you the only springs of comfort. The radiance of those thoughts which he has uttered to you, and which will live in your hearts forever, must surely turn your darkness into day. God has gathered a dark night about your hearts. But in the faith and hope of your loved child—in the triumph of his life and death—in his eternal rest and joy—he has given you a song for this night. Sweetly should you sing to the Lord of mercy and of love. True, the instruments of human melody are broken by this sorrow.— It has shattered the frame and rent the cords of your spirit's harp. No human hand can waken its melody. But God touches its strings, and they give forth music—music all the sweeter for the sorrow that has rudely swept them. This night will doubtless deepen upon you. Grief like yours is wont to grow. But your consolation may also deepen in its fulness, and your song in its sweetness. Keep near to God in this trial, and He will sustain you. He will fill your soul with singing. I point you to Him alone. As the fires of the Roman vestals when extinguished, could not be re-lighted save only at the sun, so God alone can give you light in your darkness, and joy in your grief. Be comforted therefore in Him. Cast your burdens only upon Him. He will surely sustain you. It may be that your own departed one will be the angel bearer of this blessing to your seeking souls, and that, as the heavenly calmness and the heaven-born joy go out over your spirits, you may be strangely conscious that the loved one is near you. Then look up, my weeping friends, look up! The comforts and the promises of God stud your darkened sky like stars."

CHAPTER XI.

Syracuse after Death.

---

21 But, oh! that star of the morn still gleams,
    With light to direct my feet,
  Where, when I have done with my earthly dreams,
    The mother and child may meet.

21 (241)

CHAPTER XI.

THE announcement of Scovell's dangerous illness was received in Syracuse with expressions of deep, general and heartfelt sorrow. Every message from his sick bed was anticipated with painful interest, and when at length the telegraph brought the news of his death, many a hearth side bore testimony to the sincerity and extent of the mourning which the bereavement occasioned. For Scovell was a welcome visitor in the families of his companions of the school room and play ground, and was loved far beyond the circle of his parents' acquaintance, for his gentle, manly deportment, his joyous, cheerful and happy spirit, his affectionate and generous disposition, his marked conscientiousness, and his daring ever to do right.

On the day of his death, and almost at the hour when he breathed his last breath, Rev. Mr. Talmage, from the pulpit of the Reformed Dutch Church, remembered him and his parents in a most earnest appeal to the mercy seat, that they might have strength given them in this hour of trial, and be able to submit with holy resignation to the will of God. At noon, Mr. Marshall presented Scovell's dying message, as received by telegraph, to the Sabbath school of the First Presbyterian Church, and accompanied it by most affectionate and impressive remarks. It was the first meeting of the school after a long summer vacation, and this message was from the death bed of one who was present at the last assembling, and who had been among the most punctual in attendance, and diligent in attention. His love for the school had been most ardent and constant, and was undiminished at the dying hour. On both occasions the flowing tears and heaving bosoms plainly indicated the depth of emotion, the heartfelt sorrow of all who had known the child.

On Tuesday morning, September 18th, the following article from the pen of B. B. Mahon, local editor, appeared in the columns of the "Central City Daily Courier," of which paper Scovell's father was the editor:

"MISSING.—A bright, black-eyed child, whose sweet voice caroled with the birds in the Eden of life's morning—whose busy hands caught the sunbeams and wove them into garlands for the parent's brow, is missing!—is missing! While here, angels came and whispered 'Innocence' in his ear, and earthly tongues talked of sublime simplicity. A garden of Paradise is planted in every household, and when love's guardian goes out from its blessed portals, an earthly angel is missing! All along the rough path that leads on among the thorns and thistles, we follow the foot prints of our angel, but only shadows lie darkly where the sunbeams once nestled lovingly, and though we are forever calling for our angel to come back to us, our darling is missing! *Missing!* Oh, what volumes of agony in that word! Wonder

21*

if the angels know what an agony of grief stirs the fountains of the soul—wonder if they wept when the sweet confidence went out from parental hearts, when they lost the blessed trust of childhood—wonder if it be they who come and talk with the agonized at times, fanning the fevered brow with their white wings, and whispering of the New Jerusalem, while the mourners sit beneath the weeping willow thinking of the missing one. Missing!—a boy whose eagle eye looked ever far away up to the purple mountain tops— to the castle that Hope built of jasper, ermine and diamonds—whose bold hand was ever pointed upward—leading imagination captive over the rocks—leaping wild chasms fearlessly—calling upon his youthful followers, with clarion voice, to attempt the ascent and fear not—while the world looked on admiringly, shook its grey head ominously, and surnamed the youthful guide by the euphonious title of Ambition! Parents and friends follow him up! up! up! despite the tempest that hurls seeming obstacles in their way—even until the blinding sleet of death dashed from hands grim and withered with age, shut out every earthly hope; and when we look upon Ambition's mountain again, our angel is missing! And though sometimes we think his voice is calling to us— breaking in upon the din and bustle of life, we turn aside to catch a glimpse of him, only to find that he is missing—still missing!— Missing!—how cruel the sentence. Hopes that were fortunes—that came to us with the sunlight resting on their fair faces—some which led us through the dark paths of life's pilgrimage—paths in which, mayhap, our feet would have gone astray, had they not been buoyed up by faith and trust in our heavenly Guide. Hopes that led us on to the city of the heavenly Jerusalem, with its cooling fountains and wondrous flowers! How we clung to them—until all the world grew dark about us—till even the stars forgot to shine for us, and one particular star, the brightest in the constellation, was missing! And there are other stars missing! A bright particular star has gone out — its light upon earth is set forever! Friends, too, are missing—friends who have come and sat down at our fire-side—looked into our eyes and read the sweet thoughts of our hearts.— Many are lost to us in the tide of popular applause—the hot sun of prosperity has blinded others—and some—aye, *one*—our household angel—death can tell us of him.— He for whom our longing eyes will look in vain—through the silent chamber of the heart—in the vacant chair by the hearthstone —through the dark shadow of the grave, whose sable curtains have shut out the light of his young countenance—is missing! And now the lonely spirit sits mournfully in its weeds of sorrow, waiting for the angel of consolation to come and lift the curtain, when light shall break in among the shadows— light from the glorious land—where voices shall chant no more their funeral dirges for the missing, and where engraven in letters of gold, the drooping eyes will catch new light, and the soul new inspiration from the last message uttered by the dying one—'Be Christians—meet me in Heaven!'"

So great was the interest manifested, that this article had to be republished in order to supply the demand for copies for preservation by sympathising friends. The "Syracuse Daily Journal," "Syracuse Daily Union," and "Syracuse Daily Standard," also noticed the death in the appropriate language of genuine sympathy. We quote a paragraph from the article in the "Journal":

"We had often heard of this boy as one of great purity of character and nobleness of spirit. He was peculiarly exempt from the faults which in many cases attach to lads of his age. He was cheerful, obedient, kind to his associates, never quarrelsome. He always sided with those whom other boys undertook to thrust aside. He was one of those loving, studious, truthful, filial and devoted boys that attract the love of all with whom they come into association."

On the next Sabbath, September 23rd, Scovell's death was tenderly and appropriately announced at the opening of the First Presbyterian Sabbath school, by the Superintendent, Mr. James Marshall; whereupon his class, by their teacher, Hon. I. S. Spencer, presented a series of resolutions expressing the love and sympathy of his classmates. The resolutions were adopted by the school, and the shield of "Robert Raikes'" class directed to be "draped in mourning until our next anniversary."

Interesting and impressive remarks were made by Judge Spencer, and by Rev. Dr. Canfield, pastor of the Church, and the school closed this part of the exercises by singing the appropriate Sabbath school hymn, beginning:

> "Death has been here and borne away,
> A brother from our side!"

On the same day, at the regular session of the Reformed Dutch Sabbath school, after a few appropriate and touching remarks by the pastor, similar resolutions were unanimously adopted. The last resolution was as follows:

"*Resolved*, That the foregoing resolutions be published in the public journals of our city; that they be enrolled upon the records

of our Sabbath school, and also that a copy
be presented to the parents of the deceased."

Rev. James A. Thorne, one of the editors
of the "Oberlin Evangelist," was providen-
tially in Syracuse soon after Scovell's death.
The following extracts are taken from an
article from his pen, which subsequently appeared in that paper :

"Being invited by a kind friend to visit
the Sabbath school belonging to the First
Presbyterian Church, under the pastoral care
of Dr. S. B. Canfield, my attention was
called, soon after entering the school room,
to a row of shields suspended on the wall,
each inscribed with some motto, and a corresponding device, designative of the class
to which the shield belonged. On one was
this inscription, 'The Pearl Gatherers;' on
another, 'The Gleaners,' etc. Passing down
the aisle, reading the successive inscriptions
and observing the devices on the several
shields saw one with the name and likeness of ' Robert Raikes' upon it, and I
noticed that it was heavily draped with

mourning. The class beneath it bore the signs of sorrow. It was a class of boys. They had a sad yet chastened expression, that told of some painful affliction, but at the same time denoted that the cup of sorrow was mingled with comfort. I inquired what bereavement had befallen that class; whether it had lost its teacher, or one of its members. I was informed that a fine little boy had been recently removed from that class by a violent illness, and that the whole school was in mourning, for he was beloved by all and was an extraordinary child.

I was told that in his distressing sickness he showed wonderful faith, and joy in the prospect of dying. He was specially solicitous lest his dear mother should take his death harder than he wished her to, and he earnestly prayed that God would help her to bear it. He died in the fullness of hope in Christ, and his prayers for his mother were signally answered. His parents were in deep grief, but they were sustained and comforted by the grace of God.

Other particulars were detailed to me by the pastor's wife, my informant, such as impressed me with the remarkable piety of this boy of eleven years.   *   *   Such was the interest felt in this lovely boy, that when his funeral discourse was preached the church would not hold the people that thronged to testify their respect and sorrow."

It would be difficult to imagine and impossible to describe the sorrow which possessed the hearts of Scovell's parents as they returned childless to their desolate home.— The bereaved father, in an editorial in the "Central City Daily Courier," of September 29th, gave expression to his feelings in the following language:

"Our parental heart bleeds under the affliction, and our thoughts can with difficulty be withdrawn from a retrospective contemplation of his death bed, his coffined remains, and the narrow resting place of his body in the beautiful cemetery at St. Catharines, or from the present realization of our great bereavement.   Every object at the

22

hearth side; every picture upon the wall; the vacant chair at the table; every thing about our home, speaks of him to us continually.— There hangs his hat, and his overcoat, and his satchel filled with books, where he was wont to leave them on his coming in from school; there is the little bed beside which we have so often anxiously watched his feverish slumbers; there are his skates and his toys, his books and his drawings, just as he left them weeks ago, when joyfully he took his way to his grandfather's for a vacation visit. He shall never see them again, but they shall be continual reminders to us of past joys, of present sorrows, and of a great loss, the memories of which time can never efface."

In a previous article, from St. Catharines, he had written, in anticipation of this desolation, but had, at the same time, raised the cloud to admit the sun light of consolation and Christian comfort. He said of Scovell:

"His body lies beneath the sods in the cemetery, but his spirit has gone 'home to heaven.' The bright beaming of his eye shall no longer light our pathway in life; his merry laugh shall no more be music to our ears, and the patter of his feet upon the stairs shall not again announce his joyous coming. But he shall 'shine as the stars' to guide our journey upward; he shall sing the song of the redeemed with the angels in glory, and his feet shall eternally tread the golden streets of the New Jerusalem. A home on earth has been exchanged for mansions in the skies, the pleasures of this world for the joys of heaven, earthly parents for a heavenly Father, whose love for him is infinite, and in whose presence he shall dwell in glory forever and forever."

Expressions of warmest sympathy were received by letter and in personal interviews, from numerous friends and acquaintances. In the article of September 29th, the father referred to them, and to the attendant acts of kindness, as follows:

"Comparatively strangers, as we are, in Syracuse, a degree of heart-felt sympathy has been manifested, and sorrow mingling

with our own, has been expressed, far beyond what we had any right to anticipate.
Words can but feebly speak our appreciation of these kindly expressions, or tell how
consoling and sustaining they are to a parent's heart. They will be cherished among
our life memories of him whose early call
from earth has desolated our home and
written us childless."

The following beautiful communication was
furnished for publication in the "Courier,"
by Miss Lydia Ostram, one of the faithful
teachers in the Sabbath school with which
Scovell was connected:

> "'I shall soon drink clear water in Heaven.'
> —_Last words of Scovell H. McCollum._

Yes, 'clear water,' even that crystal
stream, flowing out from the throne. There
shall be no mingling in that cup,—nothing
earthly to dim its clearness,—neither bitterness nor taint shall detract from its sweetness;
no unsatisfied longing for something more

refreshing shall follow the drinking of that Water of Life.

Unlike earthly fountains, it shall never cease its flow,—but on through eternal ages, gushing forth from its undimished source, it shall give healing and life to unnumbered millions, whose joyous thanksgiving 'shall make glad the city of our God.' It was bitter agony for you, stricken parents, to put those clustering curls from off that fair brow, and look upon those beautiful eyes, closing for their dreamless sleep ; to feel that the heart which had been so joyous, which had throbbed so high with hope for the future, which had so thirsted after knowledge, would be pulseless now ! Did not that word of triumph — that eager looking out toward joys almost reached, bring something like balm to your breaking hearts?

It is a strange, mysterious way through which the Father's hand is leading you. He has brought you to a silent and darkened home ! Oh, what unutterable agony must surge through your hearts as you enter it again ! — the music of that ringing laughter,

22*

the sound of those rushing feet, the sunshine of that joyous spirit gone from it forever! Amid all this, comes there not a sweet melody, the echo of those exultant tones,— those glad notes so soon to swell the anthem of the redeemed?

Are not those treasured words gleams of light flashing athwart the shadows? Can you not hear that spirit voice calling to you through the gloom, 'Come this way — here safe in Heaven I am waiting for thee?'

The places are many, besides his home, from which Scovell's voice and presence will be missed;—his day school, where he rapidly acquired the knowledge he loved so well, where his manly, cheerful spirit made him beloved by teacher and school mates;—his Sabbath school, where his unfailing presence and his ever ready answers showed that he sought not earthly wisdom alone;— to his companions there came his dying message: 'Be Christians—meet me in Heaven.'

We rejoice that above the wail of anguish rises the glad shout of victory; that though we must mourn his absence here, we may, through faith, look away, even unto the Shining City where, 'safe from temptation, safe from sin's pollution,' he is now drinking 'clear water' from the 'River of Life.'

One who will miss him from his Sabbath school, writes these few sorrowing yet rejoicing words to his mourning parents.

SYRACUSE, Sept. 25, 1860."

On Friday, September 28, Mr. Marshall's school room was rendered interesting by exercises commemorative of the deceased. The badges of the two societies were draped in mourning, that of the "Delphic" by means of the tastful arrangement of black and white crape, and that of the "Clionian," to which Scovell had belonged, by means of the graceful hanging of eight black tassels, and the bordering of black cord. Upon Mr. Marshall's table stood a beautiful boquet of white flowers interspersed with myrtle.

In the forenoon, Rev. H. C. Riggs, of Potsdam, N. Y., who had stood at the bedside and officiated at the funeral, addressed the scholars, presenting the lessons of sorrow.

of joy, of consolation and of warning, to be derived from the death of their late school mate. He spoke with much feeling, making an impression both solemn and earnest.

During an intermission at noon, a meeting of the scholars was held, and appropriate resolutions were unanimously adopted.

In the afternoon occurred the regular periodical public exercises. Many affecting references were made to the death which had for the first time broken their circle, and the following beautiful obituary was read as a part of the Paper of the Clionian society:

> " ' Friend after friend departs :
> Who hath not lost a friend ? '

I deem it probable there is scarcely one of us but is familiar with these sad lines; but with what a greater depth of truthful meaning they speak to us when we are compelled to *feel* that it is one of *our* number who has just crossed the 'Dark River,' and we know is now standing on the farther glorified shore, while we must yet linger with mournful hearts upon the nearer brink, gazing into the murky blackness, striving vainly with our mortal eyes to catch just one glimpse of the vanished loved one, or a single gleam of light from the radiant land beyond.

And thus it is that now those lines remind us of a dear one departed. The death angel has entered our circle! There is a vacant seat in our school room; a merry voice and boyish form, with its handsome beaming face, missed from our sports. A talented scholar has gone from our class, and a cherished member from our society. But a few weeks since, we were saying our good-bys for the vacation, hopeful for a happy reünion, thoughtless of a broken circle; but now we have come together once more, but many miles away, with his laughing eyes forever closed, his dark, curling hair for the the last time turned back from his fair brow, and his hands meekly folded on his breast—Scovell is sleeping under the green sod of his early grave.

Beautiful, talented and loved; the only

child of doting parents, after a short illness, and trusting in that Saviour who heareth the prayers of even 'these little ones,' he fell asleep. 'The golden bowl is broken, and the silver cord loosed,' and oh, the bleeding hearts that mourn his loss! striving almost vainly through their bitter grief to lift the eye of faith and whisper, 'Not mine, but thy will be done.' God bless them!

Even in his last moments Scovell did not forget his Sabbath and day school; but to each class mate and member he left the rich legacy of a dying message fraught with the most faithful love—'Be Christians.—Meet me in Heaven.' His loving heart could not have conceived, or his young lips uttered happier advice. In the first short sentence he expressed the sum total of what our lives should be, and in the second, what is the reward of such a life, even a heavenly home. And how solemn should be to us that message uttered by dying lips! Earthly mists were vanished from his sight, and in the clear light of eternity, even as we must all of us view them, he beheld life and death. And what will be our feelings in that trying hour, if we have not the sustaining arm to support us, upon which he leaned? Then let us think of it soberly and earnestly, and see if it be not the wise course to heed his message, so when for us, as now for him, life's battle shall have been bravely fought, and we too shall have passed the 'Dark River,' and stand on 'the Shining Shore,' we shall meet him in Heaven, and sing with him, while with ravished hearts we sweep our hands over the strings of our golden harps—Hallelujah, 'Te Deum' to Christ our Redeemer!"

The exercises were closed by singing the following beautiful and appropriate verses, to the tune of "Naomi:"

> "Death has been here, and borne away
>   A brother from our side;
> Just in the morning of his day,
>   As young as me, he died.
>
> We cannot tell who next may fall
>   Beneath thy chastening rod;
> One must be first,—but let us all
>   Prepare to meet our God.

> May each attend, with willing feet,
>   The means of knowledge here;
> And wait around the mercy seat,
>   With hope as well as fear."

The following poetic tribute, from the pen of Miss Anna C. Maltbie, of Syracuse, was published in "The Courier" of September 29th:

"S. H. McC.

'A truant from time, from tears and from sin,
   The angel on watch took the wanderer in.'
                              —*B. F. Taylor.*

A truant from time, and its wearisome years,
Its valleys of shadow, volcanoes of fears,
Its dark disappointments, its surge of despair,
Its waves of commotion, its mælstroms of care.
No hope now shall set, like a star on the night:
No flower he has gathered shall fade in his sight;
No spring he may drink of to bitterness turn;
And the crown on his brow like a seraph's shall burn.

A truant from tears! then the last pang is o'er!
The wild sound of weeping he heareth no more;
With the sad kiss at parting his last tear was shed,
And earth's pain and anguish forever are fled.
No 'Bochim' he finds in the city above,
For he who came thence, full of pity and love—
The pale 'Man of Sorrows,' so tender, so mild,
Has wiped off all tears from his glorified child.

A truant from sin! then the pure heart is blest!
How his powers shall expand in the mansions of rest!
While a learner he sits at the Great Teacher's feet,
Where the wise and the good, all as scholars shall meet.
No thought of corruption on that heart shall prey!
No subtle temptation shall lead him astray!
Their waves never break on the heavenly shore;
That haven once gained, he shall wander no more.

From the home that he left, all its brightness hath fled;
The flower of the household lies faded and dead;
But hopeless ye mourn not, though brief were the years
Your darling might spend in the valley of tears.
You miss his companionship, long for his smile;
Yet, have you no cause for thanksgiving the while,
That early 'a truant from time, tears, and sin,
The angel on watch took the wanderer in?' "

On Sabbath evening, September 30th, the
Reformed Dutch Church was crowded by a
deeply sympathizing and appreciative audience, to listen to a commemorative sermon
by the pastor, Rev. T. DeWitt Talmage.—
The superintendent and most of the teachers,
and the class to which Scovell belonged,
from the First Presbyterian Sabbath school,
were present. The teachers and superintendent were seated together, and the class
23

occupied a pew directly back of the afflicted parents. And thus was concluded the last earthly demonstration of affection by the Sabbath school associates of Scovell Haynes McCollum. The sermon was a beautiful tribute to childhood, and made a deep impression upon the audience. Extracts from the concluding portion are given below:

" Now, my friends, one of the best illustrations of the beauty, and susceptibility and cheerfulness, and power of a child over the parental heart, I find in the life and death of Scovell Haynes McCollum. In addition to the ordinary attractiveness which I have said always attaches itself to childhood, there was something which would cause you to remark him in a company of a hundred; something in his eye, in his forehead, in his erectness and in his manner. While every one who ever spoke to him discovered a manliness far beyond his years, he was nevertheless a thorough *boy*, and no step was quicker, and no voice louder on the play ground than his. He was neither by nature nor culture, one of those children which seem

prematurely grave. His laughter and his
romping were but the outgushing of a boy's
heart. If he was among the first in study,
he was also among the first in play. For all
of that, he will be missed the more, now
that he is gone. I shall miss him from
yonder pew to which he loved to come, the
bright and cheerful boy. His voice will no
more be lifted in our song, nor his head
bowed with us in prayer; for he hath gone
where the Sabbath song never ceases, and
the Sabbath sun never sets. Another light
has gone out from earth, but another light
has been kindled in Heaven. * * * *

There was a sweetness and glory linger
ing about his death bed. * * * His soul
went out with a peace and gentleness which
made it seem most unlike what men call
death. * * * * * * *

There are children here to-night. Oh,
that they would hear the voice which comes
to them from the dead. You see what a
glorious thing it is to be a Christian. Come
now to Jesus. While life is bright and beautiful, like Scovell, lay yourself at Jesus' feet.

Religion will take no joy from your heart, nor spring from your step, nor sparkle from your eye. Religion's ways are ways of pleasantness, and all her paths are peace.

* * * * * * * * *

Warm shall be the greeting after so sad a parting. Mothers!—your little ones shall hear your voice and come rushing down from their thrones to heaven's gate to greet you in, gladder than ever at the door of your earthly homes they welcomed you back from a journey. Parents and children, husbands and wives, friends and lovers scattered at the grave, but gathered again in the heavens.— Oh! how we shall gather them up! Before we look at the temples, before we listen to the songs, before we drink of the fountain, before we walk under the trees, before we rise upon our thrones, we shall cry, 'Where are the loved and the lost?' and then how we shall gather them up: oh! how we shall gather them up!"

Mrs. John B. Burnett, of Syracuse, from the depths of a heart prepared for sympathy

by its own bereavements, gave expression to
her feelings in the following selected lines:

"PASSING UNDER THE ROD. *

[Lines respectfully dedicated to the afflicted
parents, as a token of the heartfelt sympathy
of a friend who has 'passed under the rod.']

I saw the young bride in her beauty and pride,
  Bedecked in her snowy array,
And the bright flush of joy, mantled high on her cheek,
  And the future looked blooming and gay;
And with woman's devotion she laid her fond heart
  At the shrine of idolatrous love,
And she anchored her hopes to this perishing earth,
  By the chain which her tenderness wove.
But I saw when those heart strings were bleeding and torn
  And the chains had been severed in two,
She had changed her white robes for the sables of grief,
  And her bloom for the paleness of woe.

* It was the custom of the Jews to select the tenth of
their sheep, after this manner. The lambs were separated from their dams and enclosed in a sheep cote, with one
narrow way out. On opening the gate the lambs hastened to join their dams, and a man placed at the entrance
with a rod dipped in ochre, touched every tenth lamb,
marking it with his rod, saying, 'Let this be holy.'
  23*

But the Healer was there, pouring balm on her heart,
　　And wiping the tears from her eyes,
And he strengthened the chain he had broken in twain
　　And fastened it firm to the skies.
There had whispered a voice, 't was the voice of her God,
　' I love thee, I love thee! pass under the rod.'

I saw the young mother in tenderness bend
　　O'er the couch of her slumbering boy,
And she kissed the soft lips as they murmured her name,
　　While the dreamer lay smiling in joy.
Oh! sweet as a rose bud encircled with dew,
　　When its fragrance is flung on the air,
So fresh and so bright to the mother he seemed
　　As he lay in his innocence there.
But I saw when she gazed on the same lovely form,
　　Pale as marble, and silent, and cold;
But paler and colder, her beautiful child,
　　And the tale of her sorrow was told.
But the Healer was there, who had smitten her heart,
　　And taken her treasure away;
To allure her to heaven he had placed it on high,
　　And the mourner will sweetly obey.
There had whispered a voice, 't was the voice of her God,
　' I love thee, I love thee! pass under the rod.'

I saw when a father, and mother, had leaned
　　On the arms of a dear, cherished son,
And the star in the future, grew bright to their gaze
　　As they saw the proud place he had won,

And the fast coming evening of life promised fair,
　And its pathway grew smooth to their feet,
And the starlight of love glimmered bright at the end,
　And the whispers of fancy were sweet.
But I saw when they stood bending low o'er the grave,
　Where their hearts' dearest hope had been laid,
And the star had gone down in the darkness of night,
　And the joy from their bosoms had fled.
But the Healer was there, and his arms were around,
　And he led them with tenderest care,
And he showed them a star in the bright upper world,
　'T was their star, shining brilliantly there—
They had each heard a voice, 't was the voice of their God,
　' I love thee, I love thee I pass under the rod.'

SYRACUSE, Sept. 30, 1860.　　　　　　　　　B."

LINES KINDLY DEDICATED TO THE AFFLICTED PARENTS.

BY J. W. BARKER.

" ' I shall soon drink clear water in Heaven.'
　　　　　　　　—*Scovell's last words.*

　　' Weep not, mamma, I 'm going home ;
　　　　It is not far away ;
　　　Just o'er this dark and turbid stream
　　　　Shines an eternal day ;
　　And I can hear the silver rills
　　That murmur down the glowing hills.

Soon I shall quench my raging thirst
   From streams that never dry,
And pluck sweet fruitage from the bowers
   Whose blossoms never die;—
Nay, 'tis not dying thus to go
From this dark world of sin and woe.'

'But we shall miss thy cheerful voice
   At morn and blushing eve,
And at the memory of thy love
   Our stricken hearts will grieve;
Thy presence ne'er again will cheer
The shadows of life's waning year. .

Lonely will be our quiet home,
   Since thou art gone away,—
Cheerless the dark and voiceless eve,
   And long the weary day;
O! wilt thou never, never come
To cheer the darkness of our home?'

'O! cease thy weeping, mother dear;
   That shining land of bliss,
Just rising o'er the swelling flood,
   Is very near to this;
Only this dark and chilly stream
Is flowing silently between.

I'll visit thee, on shining wings,
   At eventide and morn,

And whisper to thy weary heart
    Sweet words when I am gone.
In answer to thy fervent prayer,
Sweet messages of love I'll bear.

    Dear papa, I am going home
        A little time before:
    O! I shall greet you very soon
        Upon that shining shore.
A few more days of joy and pain,
And we shall meet, in heaven, again.'

    As passed the loving spirit o'er
        The 'dim and shadowy vale,'
    The glorious residents of bliss
        . The new-born spirit hail.
Forever more a quiet rest
Is found upon the Saviour's breast.

BUFFALO, September, 1860."

CHAPTER XII.

Effect on Fulton Street Prayer Meeting.

News of Death.—Testimonies.—Triumphant Grace.—
Published Account.—Influence on Public Mind.—
Christians made to Pray.—More Faith in Prayer.—
The Priceless Piece of Paper—Thanksgivings.—Ef-
fect Abiding.—Christians Moved to New Hopes.—
Spirit Dispensed to Children.—Their Requests in the
Meeting.—Conversions.—The Angel Preacher's Minis-
try Begun.

DAYLIGHT IS GOING.

"Daylight is going "—
'T will soon be past.
Shadows are lengthening,
Lengthening fast!
Swiftly the moments fly,
Seize them, while passing by,
Work, work, the night draws nigh;
Work, to the last!

(275)

CHAPTER XII.

THE intelligence of Scovell's death came into the Fulton Street Prayer Meeting some time during the last eight or ten days of October, 1860. On the first day of November appeared in the "New York Observer" a sketch of the last hours of this dear boy, written by his father, setting forth the dying exercises and testimonies of Scovell, to the sustaining and triumphant grace which was vouchsafed to him during the last few days of his life. This was eagerly read by thousands of children. Parents read the touching narrative at their firesides, and superintendents in their Sabbath schools. The dying charge of this little boy to his Sabbath school mates—" Be Christians; meet me in heaven," was often repeated in the ears of listening children, in various parts of the land. The story of his last trials and triumph was told in many a prayer meeting, and Christians were moved to pray with unwonted fervor and faith for the conversion of the young all over the country. The effect of the death of Scovell upon the Fulton Street Prayer Meeting was very marked and decided. Many, very many of those accustomed to attend these meetings remembered how the meeting was moved, when Scovell's request for prayer was first presented to it. Often, during many ensuing weeks, was he made the subject of earnest supplication, and though his name was forgotten, "the little Syracuse boy" had offered for him many a prayer, which, we have no reason to doubt, went up from earnest believing hearts.

Months had passed and we heard no more from the child, and knew not that we should ever hear from him again.

One morning, on one of the last days of October, a gentleman arose in the meeting, holding a piece of paper in his hand, and said:

" I suppose no amount of silver and gold would be sufficient to buy this little piece of of paper. There is a wonderful history connected with it. Mr. Chairman will you allow me to read it to the meeting? It is as follows :

'MARCH 18th, 1860.

To the Fulton Street Prayer Meeting :

I have heard that persons might ask for prayers. I thought you would be so kind as to pray for me, a little boy of ten years, that I may be converted.

SCOVELL H. McCOLLUM,

Syracuse, N. Y.

P. S.—*Pray* for me every day.'

I took this from the Book of Requests in the upper lecture room and left a transcript of it in its place. I have spent hours in looking for it. This is wanted, to be returned to his parents, who seek it as part of the history of an only son and an only child, and a most precious chapter in that little life. On the 16th day of September last, this little boy soared away to his everlasting rest in heaven.

He died a most triumphant death by faith in Jesus Christ. I remember when that request was read in this meeting, and how it took hold on all our hearts. I remember the earnest prayers which we offered up. We cannot tell whose prayers were answered. This very request is a prayer — for there was the deep desire to be converted in that young heart. It may be it was this, or ours, or his parents' prayers which were answered. It may be that it was the prayers of all, united and combined, that called down such wonderful blessings upon this little boy, and procured the manifestation of such amazing grace in the dying hour. But sure it is, that prayer was answered, and a little lamb has been gathered into the bosom of the good Shepherd. What a history is connected with this little piece of paper! No wonder that silver and gold cannot buy it. We keep the copy. We send the orginal to those who will shed many tears of joy and sorrow when they see these lines."

Rev. Dr. Newell, pastor of the Allen Street Presbyterian Church, who was, for that day,

the leader of the meeting, remarked that he was well acquainted with the father of this little boy, who was the editor of a daily paper in the city of Syracuse, and that this meeting is called upon to render devout thanksgiving to God, for this instance of the Gospel's saving power, and for this signal answer to prayer. Let every parent, said he, and every Sabbath school teacher, and every one, who has the care of children and youth, be encouraged by this manifestation of divine mercy, to prayer and effort for the salvation of the young.

An Episcopal clergyman immediately followed these remarks, pouring out the heart-felt gratitude of the meeting, in humble praise to God for his converting grace, bestowed upon this little boy, in answer to prayer, and remembering with earnest supplications the bereaved parents, that they might be comforted with all spiritual consolations in Jesus Christ. Then a Presbyterian minister followed in another prayer, in the same strain of gratitude and joy and earnest thanksgiving.

24*

Meantime almost every eye in the meeting was overflowing with the falling tears, and after it was closed, many came forward, wishing for themselves to see the handwriting of the little boy, and some to get a transcript of the request to bear with them to their distant homes.

We think we have rarely seen the meeting so moved as when the intelligence was communicated that Scovell Haynes McCollum had left behind him such clear and convincing evidence that he had been converted, and that he had now gone home to be—

"Forever with the Lord."

The influence upon the meeting was not fleeting and evanescent, but abiding. Children—our children—all children were prayed for as we had rarely ever heard them prayed for before. A tender chord of sympathy had been touched, which vibrated through all hearts—not only in this meeting, but in many other prayer meetings in New York and its surroundings. Christian fathers and mothers, Christian pastors and Sabbath school teachers, felt themselves stirred up to animated earnestness in prayer and supplication in behalf of the young.

Many felt that children had been too much overlooked and neglected, and our faith in regard to their conversion had been too vague and shadowy and feeble. A great change was evidently taking place under the power of this shining example. Men prayed in earnest, and believed as well as prayed.— The conversion was a subject of frequent remark and appeal, and Christians confessed how unbelieving they had been, and how cruel that unbelief was.

A great change had come. For days and weeks the meeting was overshadowed by a heavenly influence, and a greater burthen than any other seemed to be an overwhelming desire for the salvation of children.— Those who attended the meeting through the closing months of 1860 and the first months of 1861 will not soon forget them, as characterized with this earnestness of desire for the outpouring of the Holy Spirit upon our children and youth, and for their conversion.

Many felt that the set time for the dispensation of the Spirit to children *had come*, and they prayed as if they expected that a great ingathering was to be made of the lambs into the fold of the good Shepherd. It was known that of late years great numbers of children had been converted. But no such general work of grace had been seen as the people of God now desired to witness.

Soon requests from children for prayers for their conversion began to flow into the Fulton Street Prayer Meeting from different and distant portions of the country.

It was no spasm—this movement among children and for them. It was the result of no human contrivances or human instrumentalities. A little boy had died—away in Canada West— remote from this sacred place of prayer, who had been consecrated to the work of the holy ministry of reconciliation, by a whole lifetime of prayer on the part of pious parents in his behalf. By a thousand acts of consecration that child had been devoted to the mission of preaching "the glorious Gospel of the blessed God." A father's

prayers and a mother's tears and entreaties
were poured out that God would make the
dear boy a herald of salvation, in His own
good time. The fond parents longed to have
the time come when they should see him in
the pulpit, clothed and adorned with the
badges and qualifications of the ministerial
office, his great work to be to win souls to
Jesus Christ.   God was answering prayer
in His own way, and the holy ministry of
the angel preacher was already begun.

While the hearts of these mourning, sorrowing parents were bowed under a load of
overwhelming distress, on account of their
dreadful bereavement, God was owning the
consecration which had been made, and answering the prayer which had been offered,
by making his triumphant death the voice
which should call a multitude of dear little
children from spiritual death to spiritual life,
and prepare them to sit together in heavenly
places in Christ Jesus. The power of that
death-bed scene, in St. Catharines, was made
to be felt by hundreds and thousands of
hearts all over this land, and even in foreign

lands. What was a cup of bitter sorrow to many fond hearts, which clung with unusual tenacity to this dear, gifted boy, was to be a cup of salvation to many ready to perish.— The work of grace was going on, under the guidance and power of the ever blessed Spirit, even while the mourners thought of little but their sorrow.

CHAPTER XIII.

Effect on Children.

"Daylight is going"—
How quickly now!
Life's deep, deep shadows
Fall on the brow.
Swiftly the moments speed,
Take thou of them good heed,
Each moment thou dost need—
Work, quickly now!

CHAPTER XIII.

THE movement in the Fulton Street Prayer Meeting, in respect to prayer for the conversion of children, was followed immediately by a corresponding movement among children themselves. In many neighborhoods, in many families, in many Sabbath schools, little children were inquiring what they should do to be saved. This condition of religious anxiety was met with no little incredulity on the part of Christians, who were slow to believe that young children can be converted. The first published account of the triumphant death of Scovell Haynes McCollum had gone the rounds of the religious press, not only in this country, but in England, Scotland, and Ireland. It is but a short time since a young man, lately return-

25

ed from Scotland, addressed the Fulton
Street Prayer Meeting, giving interesting
and cheering accounts of the work of grace
among children in the Old World, at the
same time that there was such a gracious
movement among children in the New.
He said that the revival among the young
was as remarkable there as here.   He described the meetings which were held for
them as full of the most intense interest.—
He said that sometimes, in going to a church
in the evening, it would be filled with child
ren—the center, from the pulpit to the far-
thest wall densely packed with the young of
all ages and both sexes.   Children cannot be
made thus to go, unless there is some great
impelling cause.   They had found out that
religion was for them as well as for those in
more advanced years.   It has been to hundreds and thousands of children in Scotland
a day of salvation—a day of feasting and
gladness.   Children were recognized as en-
titled to the promised blessings of the Saviour
of sinners—they coming to him by repentance and faith.

In the first months of 1861, in this country, this revival interest had become very general and wide spread. We heard of frequent conversions in answer to prayer. It is now thought that many hundreds of children gave abundant evidence of having passed from death unto life. We speak within bounds when we record it to the glory of infinite rich grace in Christ Jesus our Lord.

At first it was feared, that, as children are largely the creatures of imitation, much of the work that appeared would turn out to be the effect of that influence. The more cautious of the religious papers of the day spoke of this religious movement among children with much hesitation and apprehension. They would hardly credit what was daily witnessed.

All written requests for prayer, presented to the Fulton Street Meeting, are preserved in the upper lecture room for future inspection and reference. We have taken some of these without any endeavor at selection, and just as we found them, without the alteration of a word. Our readers will probably be surprised to see how clearly they prove that they were not the result of imitation; they are so unlike each other and so unlike any original. These were mostly sent to the Meeting in the early part of the winter of 1860 and 1861. We think that a careful perusal of these requests will show that these dear children were moved to make them by a power which is above all human power. It will also be seen that they came from a wide range of country.

"A little boy earnestly desires the prayers of Christians in the Fulton Street Meeting, that he may now become a true Christian, and love Jesus with all his heart.

This little boy is eight years old, and was led to make this request, by hearing the account of little Scovell of Syracuse.

HIS MOTHER."

"NEW YORK,
Five Points House of Industry.

Will the brethren at the Fulton Street Meeting please to pray for the writer of this,

that I may be truly converted and saved.—
Also for my father and mother—both unconverted—that they become good Christians."

"Brooklyn.

A little girl, twelve years old, wants very
much to be a Christian. Will the members
of the Fulton Street Prayer Meeting pray
for her?"

"San Francisco, Cal.

To the Fulton Street Prayer Meeting:

I wish that you would pray for me, a little boy of eight years. Pray for my soul.—
Pray that I may be a Christian.

A. H. W."

"A youth from one of the northern cities,
now residing in California, desires that the
Fulton Street Prayer Meeting will earnestly
implore God to hear and answer the many
prayers offered for his conversion, by his departed parents—himself feeling the need of
a Saviour. An Orphan Boy."

25*

The following was written in Roman capital letters:

"TROY, June 27, 1861.

To the Fulton Street Prayer Meeting:

Please pray for me daily, that I may become a Christian—while I am seven years old—and a useful man.   COLIN."

"PORT ROYAL, Pa.

To the Brethren of the Fulton Street Prayer Meeting:

I fervently ask your prayers on behalf of my conversion—a lad, of fifteen years—and also for my sister, who is younger than myself. Pray that God will pour out His Spirit upon a revival here, which is now going on in the two Churches. The number of converts now are about 300, of which 200 have expressed their hope in Christ."

"Twenty-three boys, in a class in a Sabbath school in a southern city, unite in asking an interest in the prayers of the Fulton Street Meeting. They are at present all unconverted."

"VIRGINIA.

A little girl is anxious for the prayers of the Fulton Street Prayer Meeting, that she may be a Christian, and also her brother."

"A little girl nine years of age wishes to be prayed for, that she may become a devoted child of the Lord Jesus Christ.

Thursday,
Brooklyn."

"A little girl — eight years — desires the prayers of this Meeting that she may have the Saviour for her father, as she has lost her earthly one."

"NEW YORK.

To the Fulton Street Prayer Meeting:

A little boy requests an interest in your prayers, that God would forgive his sins, give him a new heart, and make him a Christian."

"NEW YORK.

To the Fulton Street Prayer Meeting:

I ask you all to pray for me ; I am a young girl sixteen years of age and out of Christ. Do, for God's sake, do.   R. S. G."

The following was written in capital Roman letters, because the child was unable to write otherwise:

"Will your please pray for a little boy six years old—to make me a Christian—and for my two little sisters—four and eight— that we all may give our hearts to the Saviour.   CHARLIE."

"*To the Fulton Street Prayer Meeting:*

I am a little boy nine years old; will you please pray that God will give me a new heart and I be a Christian.   Please pray for me every day.   CHARLIE."

The following request was penned by a father at the earnest solicitation of his little son:

"*To the Fulton Street Prayer Meeting:*

Will you please pray for me, a little boy seven years old, that Jesus would now take away my wicked heart, and make me a Christian, and if it is his holy will, to grant that I may live to be a minister of the Gospel.   FREDDIE."

"BROOKLYN.

A little girl, aged eleven years, who earnestly desires to be a Christian, begs the prayers of the Fulton Street Prayer Meeting, that she may become one of Christ's lambs."

"BALLSTON, N. Y.

Will you pray for a little girl nine years old, that God may give me a new heart and that I may become a Christian.

LOUISE."

Before closing this chapter we must add some facts. In the month of December, 1860, an article appeared in one of the religious papers of the city, which speaks of the conversion of twenty children, since the death of the little Syracuse boy. It says, scores and hundreds of little boys and girls have heard it all over the land, scarcely a mail coming, which does not bring to the Fulton Street Prayer Meeting evidence of this. This is not all: many a young heart has bowed to the glorious truths which sent joy, and gladness, and salvation into the bosom of this dying boy. A writer, speaking of the conversion of thirty persons in the upper part of the city, says that eight are children.

WHAT HAPPENED IN A RAIL ROAD CAR.

The leader of the Meeting was a well-known merchant of this city. "Much has been said and written of late," said he in opening the meeting, " of the conversion of children." (He stood holding a request for prayer from a little girl in his hand). " Let me tell you what happened a few days ago in a rail road car. I was traveling over the mountains in Pennsylvania, and, sitting on a seat with a lady, we got to conversing upon the subject of religion, and especially upon the religious interest among children. She said to me:

'Do you see that little girl sitting over in yonder seat alone?'

I answered, 'Yes.'

'Well, that is my niece. She is only ten years old. I wish you would go and talk with her.'

I went and took my seat beside her, and I must confess to you that I have rarely had a more delightful half hour in my life than I had with that little girl. I found that about a fortnight before I met her she had become a Christian, and now she was full of peace and joy."

One day last week, a little boy arose and said :

"Friends of the Fulton Street Meeting, I have been for some time seeking after Christ; and now I hope I have found him. I want you to pray for me that I may be upheld by him, and that he will keep me from falling into any sin or snare."

We quote again from the book of requests:

"DECEMBER 24TH, 1860.

To the Fulton Street Prayer Meeting :
It is at the request of my dear little boy of eight years that I now address you. He has been quite desirous, for several months, to be remembered in that dear sacred place,

the Fulton Street Prayer Meeting,—more so, since reading the interesting account of Scovell Haynes McCollum, of Syracuse. On Friday morning last, he awoke in great distress, saying, 'Oh, mamma, I dreamed that God would only let me have one more day, and I was so wicked, I must be turned into hell; and I was so wretched!'

I said to him—'Can you think of any thing you can do to be saved from that dreadful place?'

He said—'Oh! yes. God will hear me if I pray to him.'

He did pray earnestly for a new heart—that his sins might be washed away—and that he might be cleansed in the blood of Christ. He said he felt better after he had prayed. I prayed for him as fervently as my unworthly lips could utter."

" MIDDLEBURY, VT., JAN. 10, 1861.

My Dear Brethren—A dear little daughter, nearly eight years old, and a son in his tenth year, have been very anxious for two or three weeks that I should write to the

Fulton Street Prayer Meeting and ask prayer for them. They have for a long time been deeply interested in the reports of the meeting given from week to week. I will give you the little daughter's request in her own words.

'Ask them to pray fervently, and not to stop praying until we are converted, for we wish to become Christians now.' "

Then there was another request from our neighboring city, Brooklyn, for prayer for two older children—a boy of 16 and a girl of 14, brother and sister—that they might be converted.

" APRIL 24TH, 1861.

The parents of a little boy ten years old, have been in the habit of reading the reports of the Fulton Street Prayer Meeting to their children, who have been much interested particularly in the conversion of children. The eldest, a daughter of twelve years, we hope has given her heart to the Saviour.

A few nights since, the boy spoken of
26

above, came from his room, about a half-hour after retiring, in great distress of mind, on account of his sins; and, while unburdening his mind to his mother, told her, that of late he had been unable to sleep because he felt that he was so sinful, and wished her to send a request for prayer to the Fulton Street Prayer Meeting, that he might become a Christian."

TESTIMONY OF A LITTLE BOY.

A boy about 12 years old, said that he wished to ask prayer for two brothers that they may be converted. He said he hoped he had within a short time become a Christian. He found the service of Christ to be his great delight. He loved the place of prayer. He could not bear that his brothers should remain away from Christ, and be without hope and God in the world.

CHAPTER XIV.

Effect on Sabbath Schools.

FACTS OF SALVATION ALWAYS ELOQUENT.—SABBATH SCHOOLS
AROUSED.—REPORTS IN THE FULTON STREET PRAYER
MEETING.—SABBATH SCHOOL SCHOLARS IN DISTRESS.—
SCHOOLS TURNED INTO PRAYER MEETINGS.—THE YOUNG
CONVERTED.—JUVENILE ASYLUM.—CHILDREN ASKING
PRAYERS.—STRONG PLACE BAPTIST CHURCH.—LAYING A
CHILD INTO THE SAVIOUR'S ARMS.—BOY.—VERY WICKED.
—WANTS HELP.—GETS IT.

"Daylight is going!"
The sun sinks low;
Work now is burdensome,
The pulse beats slow.
Life's sands are nearly run,
Life work is nearly done,
Night cometh swiftly on—
How soon, none know!

CHAPTER XIV.

NOTHING is so eloquent on the subject of salvation as the eloquence of facts. If the influence of Scovell's death was great, as a means of the conversion of children, considered in individual cases, it was much greater considered in bands and organizations as in the. Sabbath school. To show this, we quote from accounts of the Fulton Street Meeting published in the religious press.

A gentleman stated, " that so earnest had appeared the spirit of inquiry among the children and youth of the Sunday school, that the pastor and teachers thought best to turn the Sunday school exercises of last Sunday afternoon into a prayer meeting. The parents were invited, and the body of the church was crowded.

26*

Many have obtained a hope of pardon through Jesus Christ. I had good reason to be thankful, for one daughter and two sons were among the number who were seeking the Lord. That night my house was a Bochim — a place of tears. But oh! what joy when we gathered for family worship next morning. There was I, who had walked for years alone, and that daughter, and two sons, all rejoicing in the joys of pardoned sin. One daughter — the only other child — remained out of the ark of safety. She was in great distress of mind. She, too, has since found deliverance and peace."

Many of those children and some of those parents are now hopefully converted.

"In the Strong Place Baptist Church, Brooklyn, there is in progress a most glorious revival of religion. Great numbers of young people, especially, flock to the meetings. Large numbers of children in the Sabbath schools connected with the Church, are inquiring with interest what they shall do to be saved."

"Mr. Pardee, agent of the American and

New York Sunday School Union, said : It is
a time of uncommon and most manifest dis-
play of the power of the Holy Spirit among
the young of our city and the neighboring
cities. ·It is probably true that in many of
our Sunday schools there are many anxious
scholars.   Yesterday, the first school I went
into, the superintendent told me that twelve
of his pupils had lately become hopefully
pious, and that many in the school were
awakened.

'Do you see,' said another superintendent, 'those three girls on the seat there?'

I said, ' Yes.'

'Well, their teacher has just been to me,
to tell me that they are now hope that they
have become Christians.'

We have 450,000 in this city under 20,
which is more than half of our entire population, and the tables of other cities will give a
similar majority of population as being under
20 years.   It becomes, then, all who would
do any thing to save those 'who are ready
to perish,' to improve this day of merciful
visitation to the young, of the influences of
the Holy Spirit."

A writer to the Fulton Street Meeting says:

"On the first Sabbath of the month, after relating to the school an account of the triumphant death of Scovell H. McCollum, I requested all who desired an interest in Jesus, to remain for the purpose of prayer and religious conversation. 'Seven remained. Last Sabbath I repeated the invitation and the number was increased seven fold, forty-nine remaining. Pray especially for these forty-nine, that they may be led of the Spirit to give their hearts to Jesus Christ."

A gentleman said: "I was at the Juvenile Asylum. I was told that one night so many of the children were in distress of mind, that the watchman told them that as many as wished religious conversation might go down into the superintendent's room. About forty went down.

On Tuesday night a much larger number went down; and on Wednesday night the number of anxious children was so great, that after family worship the superintendent told them, that as many as were anxious about their souls might remain in the chapel. Out of the 450 to 500 children, 300 remained.

The sight would have moved any heart. After some further instruction had been given, we then said to them, that perhaps some of those boys might desire to pray, and if they did, they might then have the opportunity. Sixteen of those boys led in prayer."

Another, said : "On the first Sabbath in March, more than forty adults and children— mostly children—made a public profession of religion, and sat down together to celebrate the Lord's Supper."

A gentleman said: "A few weeks ago I was in the meeting and asked prayer for a Sunday school in the interior of Pennsylvania. To-day I am here to tell you how prayers have been answered. Almost immediately a revival began in the school, and many have been converted. Two of the converted little children have died in the triumphs of Christian faith, and have gone home to the glory of heaven. They left behind the sweetest, most precious testimony of their faith in Jesus."

The following touching narrative is referred to in the .first chapter of this book. The father of the little girl bears testimony to the influence of the simple story of Scovell's faith and triumphant death, as heard in her Sabbath school, in forming her beautiful religious character, and making her a subject of renewing grace a short time before her death.

"'FATHER, WHEN WILL JESUS COME?'

So said a little girl—a dear Sunday school scholar—to her weeping father, as he stood bending over her. It was a dreadful trial to him to ▉▉▉ his precious little daughter lie there. ▉▉▉thing her life away—to be with him no more.

'Father, when will Jesus come?' the dying little girl again repeated.

'We must wait with patience his time, my daughter,' was the sobbing reply of the father.

'Yes, we will,' was the meek rejoinder of the submissive child.

This little girl was about eleven years of age. She had the advantages of faithful parental instruction and Sunday school teaching. She was a docile little child. She drank in the lessons of the hour with an humble, earnest spirit. In the recent religious interest among children she had been one of the first to feel the power of the Divine Spirit upon her heart, and she had, among others and with some of her companions, fled for refuge to lay hold of the hope set before her. She had taken sanctuary in Jesus. She was now about to be called away from her Brooklyn home to her glorious home on high.

She had not a shadow upon her believing, trusting heart. Not a doubt disturbed her. She was only anxious that Jesus should hasten his coming.

Her sickness was very sudden. Her coming to the gates of death was entirely unexpected by herself and the family. The summons had come as a thief in the night. The disease had made short work. It had been very severe, as well as hasty.

When the superintendent of the Sunday
school called upon her, on first hearing of
her prostration, he asked her if she believed
and could trust in Jesus as her own Saviour?
She answered with seeming surprise at
such a question: 'Why, yes! Why not trust
him?'

When the physician's skill, and all that
kind, loving hearts could do, failed and
proved utterly unavailing to arrest or remove
disease, it was announced that her stay on
earth would probably be short. With much
composure she replied:

'I would like to stay a little longer with
mother, but if God wishes me to go now, I
think he will make me a little angel.'

As time flew on, her parents and grand-
parents, brothers and sisters, were all called
into her room.

After bidding them all good-bye, and
kissing them, and telling them, one and all,
to meet her in heaven, she asked her father
to read a chapter in the Bible and to pray
with her, which he did. She wished, also,
some of her beautiful Sunday school hymns

to be sung, and she endeavored to sing with the others, but her voice failed her.

When the death angel seemed to be hovering near to cut the brittle thread of life, her father knelt down to commend her spirit to God, and, while on his knees praying, a convoy of angels came and conveyed little Josephine to her happy home in heaven."

A Virginia clergyman said he had been laboring a short time in his father's old parish, in Oneida county, in this State, where there had been from two hundred to two hundred and fifty conversions, twenty of whom were children.

A man from Newark, N. J., said that in the Church to which he belonged, there had been upwards of sixty conversions—twenty-five of them being children. In several of the Churches of Brooklyn there have been of late some hopeful conversions, and most of them, in some Churches, were between 8 and 15 years of age.

From another place information was given of the conversion of 20 boys, all members of the same Bible class, and all making public

27

profession of religion, and sitting down to the table of the Lord on the first Sabbath in March.

From another place similar intelligence was received in regard to the conversion of 17 members of one Sabbath school.

A business man said : "Last December, the 31st day, just as the sun was setting, I laid my little son, six and a half years old, from my arms over into his Saviour's arms; and he took him up to heaven. He had read, with the most intense interest, the story of Scovell Haynes McCollum, and died in the same intelligent triumphant faith in Jesus Christ, assured that he was going to be forever with the Lord."

Another speaker, said: "Last Sunday afternoon we turned our Sabbath school into a prayer meeting. Seventeen of the scholars arose for prayer. Oh!" said he, "I wish you all could have been there. You would have felt that God had heard and was answering prayer. We have some hopeful conversions."

Very nearly at the same time, a gentleman

standing in the door-way, having no chance to get in, said: "I have a message to bear to this meeting. Last Sunday I was at the Juvenile Asylum, near the High Bridge. When the children were all assembled, I read to them the story of Scovell Haynes McCollum. Oh! you should have seen, as I did, the tears stealing down the cheeks of those dear children, as I read that melting and wonderful story."

A gentleman said: "I must ask for your prayers. But let me tell you for what. I have asked you to pray for my Sunday school class. Last night I heard four of those lads telling what the Lord had done for them, in their conversion. Two others are awakened."

Again, many are turning to the Lord. Whole Sabbath schools send for prayer. Whole Sabbath school classes are presented by their teachers as the subjects of prayer.

The vice superintendent of the Lee Avenue Sabbath school, now numbering 2,200 scholars, came into the meeting and related some most touching facts, which had transpired in connection with their school, and asking that the school might be made the subject of special prayer.

A gentleman spoke of a little boy, 13 years old, who came to the rooms about 9 o'clock in the morning. He was a fine looking, intelligent lad, with a look of quiet anguish on his face, and seemed to be in a great hurry.

"Can you tell me, sir," said he, "where the minister is?"

"What minister?"

"The minister who leads this Meeting every day."

"What do you want of him?"

"I want to ask him to please ask the Meeting to pray for me, for I am a very wicked boy."

"What makes you think you are a very wicked boy?"

"I have such a wicked heart, and I do *so* want a better one."

"Now, my dear boy, what has made you feel that you are so wicked and *so* to want a better heart?"

"Well, sir, I will tell you." But his tears choked his utterance.

"Will you tell me what first aroused you to think about your wicked heart?"

"It was reading about Scovell H. McCollum, who died so happy."

"Where did you read it?"

"In the papers."

"Where do you go to Sunday school?"

"I did go to St. Ann's Episcopal Church, Brooklyn."

"Where do you live?"

"In Madison street."

"Where do you work?"

"At No. — Broadway."

He stood all this time weeping. We told him we would see that his requests for prayer were presented to the Meeting, and entreated him as soon as he got to the store to go to some private place for prayer, and give himself up to the Lord Jesus to be his forever.

Two days passed. Meantime the old superintendent of St. Ann's Episcopal Sabbath school had come to the Meeting and inquired the name of the little boy of 13 years, and when told that it was F——

27*

M——, "Oh!" said he, "I know him very well, and have known him for years;" and with great earnestness he started down Broadway to his place of business.

The day following he came into the Meeting and said: "You will all remember the case of the little boy 13 years old. Yesterday I called to see him. Oh! I wish you could have seen the smile and the peace which was on his honest face as he met me."

"Oh!" said he, "I have found Christ—I have found Christ! All is peace now."

I inquired of him "when it was that he 'first found the Saviour?"

He answered, "Yesterday noon." It was the same hour in which the Meeting was praying for him.

"Oh! thank the Lord for the conversion of my son," said one, "and pray for the conversion of a daughter. Bless the Lord, Oh! my soul."

CHAPTER XV.

Conclusion.

We have Come to it. — Aim to give Facts.—Persuasive Voice.—Salvation to Many.—The Half not told.— Guarded Statements.—Truth has Power.—All the Facts not known. — Scovell's Death a Ministry. — Prayers answered.— Not as expected.—Far beyond Faith in Asking.—The Ministry of the Dead Living.— Crown of Glory. — Day Closing.—Night at hand.— Appeal to Parents.

> " ' Daylight is going'—
> Daylight is gone !
> Night-fall has come at last,
> Day's work is done !
> Seek not to follow thou
> The soul in death laid low,
> Its fate thou canst not know—
> Is *thy* work done ?"

(819)

CHAPTER XV.

WE have come to the conclusion of this little work. It has been our effort to get the facts together and let them speak for themselves. They have a voice more persuasive than any other. It has been an object of paramount desire that these pages may be the means of doing good to children, to parents, to Sabbath schools, and to all who have the the care of children and youth. With all our diligence we may not have entirely escaped errors. We know of none. We have all confidence that truth generally pervades these pages. There has been no attempt at embellishment. There was need of none. Truth, as revealed in the experiences of converted little children, has a power to reach the hearts of others.

It cannot fail that the impression will be

made, on all candid minds, that God had great and glorious purposes to accomplish, in his sovereign mercy and grace, by answering prayer for Scovell.

The impression will be made, that God used his death as a means of grace to bring multitudes of dear lambs of the flock, into the fold of the good Shepherd. We have relied on the facts to produce this impression. It should, however, be borne in mind, that no attempt has been made to give half the facts that have been known to us — and we probably have a right to conclude that but a small portion of the facts are as yet known, and never will be, until the secrets of all hearts shall be revealed. Yet if we judge only from what is known, we must conclude that the ministry of Scovell was a wonderful ministry — this ministry of his death. How wonderfully God answered the prayers which had been offered from his very birth, that he might be made the herald of salvation! He had been consecrated to God's service by countless acts of devotion.

When the answer to prayer for his con-

version and for his ministry of salvation
came, it came in a manner all unlooked for
by his parents, and in such a way that God
should be abundantly glorified.

But God's thoughts were not as their
thoughts. He was carrying forward his
gracious designs, in the salvation of dear,
precious children. They were mourning in
secret, while our heavenly Father was setting many gems in the Saviour's diadem,
which shall be forever stars in His crown
of celestial glory. The salvation of these
children was all of wonderful grace. No
such displays of mercy and grace had been
asked. It was infinitely beyond all that had
been looked for, even in the exercise of the
most comprehensive faith.

Why should not God have his own time
and way of answering the prayer and faith
of his people? God chose to give the preacher a stand point, and give him the eloquence
of an experience of His love far beyond that
which is commonly allotted to the ripest,
oldest, most experienced Christians. Thus
the "angel preacher" was to gather up his

power for a ministry, which shall bring many sons and daughters to GLORY.

The facts narrated in this volume appeal earnestly to the hearts of Christian parents. Scovell became what he was, and was brought to his triumphant death, through the blessing of God upon the unceasing care and devotion of an earnest, praying mother. Who will not be encouraged and stimulated to like devotion, by this bright example of the faithfulness of God to all his covenanted mercies for those who love him, and for their children after them, and by the histories of redeeming love which have been recorded? Christian parents! Will you not be stirred up to earnest, believing prayer? Will you not consecrate your children anew, to the service of your heavenly Father? Will you not learn and profit by the lessons which God has taught in the death of this dear boy, that when the death angel shall call for your household treasures, you may have like comforts and consolations as have been meeted out in so much mercy to the parents of Scovell H. McCollum?

www.ingramcontent.com/pod-product-compliance
Lightning Source LLC
Chambersburg PA
CBHW060516030726
47498CB00004B/966